TOO MANY ENEMIES

Some son of a bitch shot Gringo in the head. But he knew he still had his brains, so what the hell...

He opened up with the machine gun, traversing left to right at crotch level as corn stalks toppled and unseen somebodies screamed.

He didn't stop firing. Neither did Gaston, until he'd emptied the rifle clip and reached for another. That's when he saw what was coming up from *behind* them!

He yelled, "Dick! We're surrounded!" and was still trying to reload his rifle when a huge attacker smashed Gaston with the flat of his machete.

Captain Gringo turned, groggy from loss of blood, and pulled the trigger of his Maxim. Nothing happened. The belt had been used up...

Novels by
Ramsay Thorne

Published by
WARNER BOOKS

Renegade #20

SHOTS AT SUNRISE

Ramsay Thorne

WARNER BOOKS

A Warner Communications Company

WARNER BOOKS EDITION

Copyright © 1983 by Lou Cameron
All rights reserved.

Warner Books, Inc.,
666 Fifth Avenue,
New York, N.Y. 10103

 A Warner Communications Company

Printed in the United States of America

First Warner Books Printing: September, 1983

10 9 8 7 6 5 4 3 2 1

Renegade #20

SHOTS
AT
SUNRISE

They were all to be shot at sunrise. No particular reason. None of the people locked in the cellar of the old sugar mill had done anything. But it was a long-established Nicaraguan custom that since strangers could not be friends, strangers should be shot on general principle during a civil war.

Nicaragua had been enjoying a civil war for some time now. So, earlier that evening the troops holding that particular coastal fishing village had made a routine sweep of the plaza during the evening paseo and simply rounded up everyone they didn't know personally. Since most of those they'd arrested, male or female, had only gone to the paseo to flirt as they enjoyed an after-dinner stroll, the weeping and wailing in the dank dark cellar was considerable.

Captain Gringo remained silent as he stood by one of the few barred windows level with his own chin and the walk outside their improvised prison. He wasn't looking forward to

the coming dawn with any more enthusiasm than his fellow
prisoners, but he knew it was pointless to keep on shouting he
was innocent.

The hell of it was, he and his sidekick, Gaston Verrier,
were innocent for a change. They'd been trying to make their
way low-profile down the Nicaraguan coast to Costa Rica,
when they'd made the mistake of ordering a much-needed
snack at a sidewalk cantina during the apparently peaceful
paseo time of an apparently peaceful village. They'd known,
of course, of the civil war. There was always a civil war
going on in Nicaragua. But the two soldiers of fortune hadn't
meant to get involved, this trip.

The last time they'd passed through Nicaragua they'd
found themselves fighting on the currently losing side, and
they'd never been paid for their modest efforts to restore the
balance of power between the warring cliques of Granada and
León provinces.

But, as the other prisoners kept reminding him, loudly, it
wasn't easy to stay uninvolved in local politics. He still
didn't know which side had arrested him and Gaston.
Unless they busted out of here pronto, it wasn't going to
matter at sunrise.

Captain Gringo was working on a bar as his older sidekick
scouted the depths of the soggy celler for other means of exit.
The bar the big Yank was gripping seemed solidly set in its
mortar. But the mortar was damp and moldy and you had to
try.

As he quietly threw his weight back and forth on the rusty
bar, without much luck, a shorter man in rumpled white linen
eased up to him and asked, in English, "Any luck? You're a
Yank, too, aren't you?"

Captain Gringo went on working as he regarded the stranger morosely and said, "It's like pulling teeth. It'll either give
or it won't, all at once. Where were you when they rounded

us up? I didn't notice you when they frog-marched us all over here from the plaza."

The other Anglo said, "They grabbed me at my hotel. What the hell's going on, Mister, ah . . ."

"Rogers," Captain Gringo lied, adding, "I came down here to buy raw chicle for Wrigley's of Chicago. As to what's going on, the motherfucker who seemed to be in charge said we were all suspected of some damn thing or another, and now you know as much as me. What's your tale of woe?"

"I'm a newspaper man. Covering the fighting for the Hearst syndicate. Did they take your papers, too? My name's Peterson, by the way."

"Shit, they would have taken my rubbers if I'd been carrying any. Like yourself, I stand emptyhanded and with empty pockets, and this fucking bar won't give an inch. I don't suppose they left you with a pocketknife or even a goddamn fingernail file, Peterson?"

The man shook his head and said, "They took my passport, camera, and, of course, my money. I managed to hang on to my films, though."

"Your what?"

"Camera film. The Kodak it goes in is hopefully still in my room at the hotel. But as they patted me down they overlooked the two rolls of film. I hope this muggy heat doesn't spoil it before I can find a place to get it developed. It's already exposed, and believe you me, I've got some shots worth real money, if only I could get back to civilization!"

Captain Gringo shrugged and said, "I'd settle for just getting the hell out of here. You and your dirty pictures figure to be buried in the same hole unless we can bust out of here well this side of dawn!"

"Hey, the scoop on these little rolls of film is worth at least a quarter-mill to young Willy Randolph Hearst. He hates greasers, you know, and I got shots that could bring the marines in here pronto!''

An older Hispanic came over, looking upset about something. He asked in Spanish, ''Do either of you gentlemen know for why we are caged like animals here?''

Captain Gringo shook his head and replied, ''You heard what they said when they were rounding us up this evening, señor. I don't even know which side those soldados were on.''

Peterson said, ''Beat it, pop. This is a private conversation.'' So the old man went away, sort of sobbing to himself.

Peterson said, ''Listen, if you and that little guy you're with could help me get these pictures to Willy Randolph, I could make it well worth your while. Do you have any pals here in Nicaragua who could help us?''

''Shit, Peterson, do you see anybody helping me with this fucking bar?''

''I mean if we could somehow bust out of here. Do you know anyplace we could hide out until things cool off?''

''Things never cool off in Nicaragua. They've been fighting one another since they drove the Spanish out years ago. Let's eat this apple a bite at a time, damm it! We can worry about where to run and hide if and when we get one fucking foot outside this celler!''

''Yeah, but if you and your pal escape, you'll take me along, right?''

Captain Gringo shrugged and said, ''Sure, why not? May as well take *all* these poor suckers along, if and when. But the *if* is getting iffy as hell. I just can't do a thing with these bars, and if my pal had found another part of the cave to work on he'd have come back to say so by now.''

''Yeah, I saw him snooping around the walls back there in the dark just now. What does he do for a living, Rogers?''

''He's a banana buyer, I think. We just met tonight before the big sweep made partners in misery of us all.''

"I see. I don't think taking along all these natives would be a smart move. Wouldn't they slow us down?"

"Slow us down going where? Do you like to see innocent men and women shot at sunrise, Peterson?"

"Of course not. But can your friends here in Nicaragua hide out such a big bunch?"

Before Captain Gringo could answer, Gaston came out of the darkness to join them. Gaston was older and much smaller than Captain Gringo, but he was tougher than he looked. The dapper little Frenchman regarded the world with a cynical, worldly smile, and treated it just the way it tried to treat him. He said, "It's no use. The walls are solid masonry as well as below ground level. Do we know this other gentleman, Dick?"

Captain Gringo introduced Peterson to Gaston. Gaston listened with apparent interest to the stranger's pitch. But before Peterson finished, Gaston knifed him in the aorta.

Captain Gringo had hoped Gaston had managed to hang on to the knife he carried in a sneaky collar sheath. He clapped a hand over Peterson's mouth and lowered him casually in the semidarkness to a seated position on the floor as he said quietly, "You might have waited until he got to the stinger, Gaston."

Gaston snorted in disgust as he made the dagger vanish again, saying, "They sent him to get information, not to go through the whole charade of quote, escaping with him, unquote. I am glad you could see he was merely pumping us, too, my child."

Captain Gringo hunkered down beside the sitting corpse to go through its pockets as he replied, "Hell, I learned at my dear old Uncle Gaston's knee never to trust a fellow prisoner who wasn't in the paddy wagon with me. What's this he had in his pocket?"

"I of course looked the whole crowd over as soon as we were locked in this très fatigué sugar mill tonight, in search of fellow rogues from our last visit to Nicaragua. He was not here earlier, and they have not opened the one door I know of since. What is that you have there, my ghoulish youth?''

Captain Gringo held up two rolls of tinfoil-wrapped Eastman nitrocellulose, according to the lettering, and said, ''He had these to back his con. I was hoping for a gun. Nada. But they never would have left these cigars and matches in his shirt pocket if they didn't like him a lot.''

''Merde alors, if I thought he'd been anything but a sneak sent to spy on us I would not have knifed him. What do you think they were after, Dick? Our forged IDs could not have told them who we really were, hein?''

''I guess they wanted to check us out before they shot us. Okay, we have three cigars, matches, and two rolls of doubtless worthless nitrocellulose film. This stuff's mildly explosive, isn't it?''

''Oui, but we have neither the time nor the weak place to blow up with shredded plastique this time, my old and rare. It is after midnight. The moon will soon be setting. That gives us possibly a few short hours of darkness to make it to the adorable mangrove swamps. Why are you fatiguing yourself with that solidly set iron bar, now that you have searched our friend there?''

''Do you have any better escape routes planned, you grinning old goat?''

''But of course. If that idiot had been a ghost, he would hardly have responded so favorably to a thrust under the ribs, non? Ghosts may be able to walk through walls, but police informers . . . ?''

Captain Gringo nodded and said, ''Gotcha.'' Then he called to the old man Peterson had shooed back to the nearest clump of fellow prisoners, and when the old peon was near enough for discreet conversation, the tall American whispered, ''Keep an eye on this prick and make sure nobody yells a lot about him being dead.''

''Madre de Dios! Is he dead, señor?''

"Yeah, but we don't want it to get around. He was an agente secreto they sent to question us. If we can find out how he got in or out, we'll take the rest of you with us. That won't be easy if his pals on the outside find out he's not still pumping us for information, see?"

"Ah, entiendo bien! Have no fear, señores. I, Julio Robles, stand with you to the death, and I can speak for my own friends and relations in this terrible place, so . . ."

They didn't hang around to hear the rest of the speech. Captain Gringo took the lead, feeling his way in the dark as they got farther from the moonlight through the windows up front. He started to strike a match. But that could have been dumb. He said, "There's no way through these walls of stuccoed coral blocks. Trapdoor in that wooden ceiling up there?"

Gaston said, "Oui, it's the only possible way. Let me think. The man was average height and that ceiling is, what, twelve feet above us?"

Captain Gringo reached up to grab nothing but empty darkness as he replied, "Close enough. He didn't jump either way, and a rope hanging down would be dumb."

Gaston grabbed his arm, reached out to feel the wall with his free hand, and said, "This way. There is an old sugar vat in a far corner. I wondered, idly, why they'd left it down here, upside down. It stands a good four feet off the dirt floor, in an unfrequented part of our oversized prison."

They made their way to the big inverted wooden vat. Captain Gringo couldn't see it in the dark, but when the two of them put their weight to it, the solid mass of wood didn't move. Captain Gringo put the stuff he'd taken from the dead spy in his pockets, climbed up on the vat, and whispered, "Hold it down to a roar."

Gaston could shut up if it was important. So Captain Gringo rose in the darkness until his hands were against the planks between the rafters, his head only slightly lower. He strained his ears. He heard not a sound from above. He shoved experimentally. A square trapdoor opened with little effort and not a sound on well-oiled hinges. It was just as dark up there as down here. So he couldn't see what he was getting into as he opened the trapdoor all the way and pulled himself up through the opening. As he got a knee over the edge of the secret entrance, he heard a chair squeak and a voice in the darkness whispered, "How did it go, Yanqui? Is it safe to light the lamp now?"

Captain Gringo whispered, "No!" as he got to his feet, judging where the other guy was standing or sitting and silently moving to one side as he did so. The other leaned forward in his seat and whispered, "What's the problem? Where are you, Yanqui?"

Captain Gringo didn't answer. He swung a roundhouse left from the backfield and damn near broke his hand when it connected with somebody's ear in the dark.

The effect it had on the other guy was even more damaging. Captain Gringo heard him thud to the floor by his overturned chair. So he dived on him, groped his way to the semi-conscious unknown's throat, and strangled him good until his boot heels stopped gently drumming on the boards.

By this time Captain Gringo's business associate, Gaston, had crawled up through the trap to hiss, "Not so loud, you boisterous child! What do we have here? From the sounds, one would judge you have been choking the life out of it, hein?"

Captain Gringo remained seated on the dead man's chest as he took out a match and thumbed a light. They saw Gaston was right. The uniformed Latin he'd clobbered and choked was staring at the ceiling of the little chamber with horrified eyes and a purple face. Gaston moved to the table in one corner to help himself to the gun in a shoulder rig the spy downstairs had left there before lowering himself through the trap to play games. As the Frenchman put it on under his linen jacket, Captain Gringo removed the gunbelt of the man he'd surprised, and strapped it around his own hips after rising to his feet.

He struck another match to light the lamp on the table as the first one burned down. Gaston cracked open the one door to a dark hallway and said, "Eh bien, so far so good. We are once more armed and dangerous. Put out that ridiculous species of lamp and let us tiptoe through the tulips to parts unknown, non?"

"Have you forgotten our pals in the cellar below?"

"Who could ever forget them? But what of it, Dick? They are not our kind of people. A third of them are wearing skirts."

"Yeah, and all of them figure to be shot at sunrise if we leave 'em behind. Go get 'em and herd 'em up here while I scout the situation."

Gaston started to argue. Then he shrugged and said, "Eh bien, the more of us they have to search for, the more confused they should be as we wend our weary way for the safety of the border. But do not be long, my old and idealistic. This place makes me très nervous and I do not intend to wait for you forever!"

As Gaston lowered himself back through the trap, Captain Gringo first patted down the dead officer for any other goodies, found yet more smokes, matches, and fifty U.S. dollars' worth of Nicaraguan play money, and put it aside for a rainy day. The gunbelt he'd helped himself to already had spare rounds of .44-40 for the old single-action thumb-buster.

He left the lamp where it was, for the edification of Gaston and their newfound friends, while he eased out the door and groped his way along the narrow dark corridor toward a distant illuminated window. There wasn't a sound from the rooms on either side. The troops who'd herded them into the sugar mill had obviously selected more comfortable quarters for themselves. But they wouldn't be far. Someone had to be keeping at least a casual eye on the one official entrance out front.

When he got to the grimed window he saw he was right. The window was of course at ground level, one story above the cellar. Fortunately, the dirty glass and darkness behind him conspired to hide him as he found himself staring out at a modest bonfire in the middle of a dead-end street formed by the sugar mill on one side and an L-shaped posada or wayfarer's inn on the other. The military had taken over the posada as their G.H.Q. and quarters, judging from the lights upstairs and the soldados lounging in the doorway across from him.

None of that was as interesting as the object squatting knee-high on its tripod near the fire. A Maxim heavy machine gun was aimed at the wall forming the dead end of the street. He saw now why the executions had been put off until sunrise. Some big shot intended to enjoy the novelty before breakfast. Machine guns were still rare to any armies of the late Victorian era. Down here they were probably as exciting as a bull fight.

Gaston slithered into place at his side, whispering, "The old man is keeping the others quiet in the back room. What do we have here. . . . Ah, I see the machine gun. I see the setup, too. I know what you are thinking, you violent youth. Forget it. Let's try the back way out."

Captain Gringo said, "If we had that Maxim, the odds on getting anywhere would go up a bunch, Gaston. We have two dozen people to worry about and between us only two pistols."

"Oui, but forget the damn machine gun and regard once again the tense set up! The moment one of us makes a break for that gun, those top-story windows fill with boisterous soldados, shooting down with glee, from cover! I should say when *you* try for that Maxim, since I am a rational human being, not a suicidal maniac! Before you tell me to cover you, regard it is not possible for one man with one pistol to cover at least fifteen windows and that doorway over there. Come, let us be on our way before one of those hysterical muchachas gives the show away by bursting into tears again!''

Captain Gringo took out the rolls of film Peterson had been carrying as cover for his ridiculous story. He peeled off the tinfoil, eased up the sash, and told Gaston, ''Get the others going out the back and into the trees. I'll catch up. But first I want that Maxim!''

''Eh bien, I'll cover you, but . . .''

''Damn it, Gaston, move it out! I don't *need* cover, if this works!''

''If what works? And what if it does not?''

''I still won't need cover. I'll be dead. *Go*, Gaston!''

So Gason went. Captain Gringo counted Mississippis until he figured Gaston and the others had at least a start on him. Then he opened the window wider and tossed a spool of film underhand toward the bonfire. It missed, damn it. The man in the doorway looked up, mildly curious, trying to locate the source of the faint metallic tinkles. He spotted the rolling spool and stepped out of the doorway toward it, not looking the worried American's way as Captain Gringo tossed the second roll.

It landed in the bonfire.

Nothing happened for a moment. Then the whole street was filling with billowing clouds of acrid, thick white smoke as Captain Gringo opened the window the rest of the way and forked his leg over the sill.

He couldn't see much. Nobody could, as he took a deep breath, held it, and headed for where he'd last seen the Maxim on its tripod. A gun went off at nothing in particular, and someone was shouting something dumb about poison gas as he slammed a window shut across the way.

Captain Gringo barked his shin on the machine gun,

reached down, and lifted it from its mount to swing away and run for it, with the ammo belt dragging and trying to trip him. He staggered to the sugar mill wall, groped his way to the open window, and shut it behind him after climbing through with the heavy gun cradled in his arms. He opened the petcock of the water jacket to let it drain as he staggered down the dark hallway. He had to take a breath. When he did so, he knew he'd made a mistake. Some of the nitrocellulose fumes had followed him inside and it felt like he was inhaling liquid glue laced with ammonia.

The Maxim was lighter now, since water weighs eight pounds a gallon, but he was woozy and might not have made it had Gaston not grabbed him in the dark to steady him, and said, "This way. I sent Robles on with the others. With luck they will have all run away instead of waiting for us as I told them to. What on earth did you set fire to back there? It smells like someone just burned a skunk at the stake!"

Captain Gringo was feeling better, now that he could breathe again. So he said, "Old Edison is going to have to work some bugs out of that film if he ever expects to get anywhere with those moving pictures he's working on. Can you imagine the panic in a theater if a reel of that shit ever caught fire?"

"How droll. From all the smoke I thought you had at least set fire to an entire glue factory. Here is the back entrance. Watch your adorable step with that heavy weapon. I have the belt. Let us scamper into the forest to join the other children before those soldados notice they have been robbed as well as smoked like hams, non?"

Gaston led the way across a freshly plowed field so they could leave lots of nice footprints in case their pursuers didn't have bloodhounds. Gaston said the others were waiting amid the bananas on the far side of the forty-odd acres of open ground. The sky said they were headed south. That was the first good news tonight. Costa Rica was about the only country down here that didn't stage a revolution every five minutes, and, having a stable easygoing government, it was the best place for soldiers of fortune to vacation between job offers.

Captain Gringo could see their shadows outlined in orange on the red furrowed surface ahead. The moon had set. He glanced back over his shoulder to see the sky glowing nicely above the stark black outline of the old sugar mill. He chuckled and said, "Somebody turned over an oil lamp in the confusion back there. Looks like the posada is on fire. It couldn't have happened to a sweeter bunch of guys. Did any of the others hazard an educated guess as to which side those sons of bitches are on?"

Gaston shook his head as he kept pace, carrying the end of the machine-gun belt, and explained, "The other prisoners were as surprised as we were to be caught in that sweep this evening. Some of them are Grenadists and others used to be for León. Nobody locally was très excited about it, as they thought this area was far from the war zone."

"Jesus, we've got guys on both sides waiting for us under the bananas?"

"One hopes not. With luck, most will have run away by now. Those troops took no names as they herded us all in that cellar to await our doom. If I were a peon who'd just gone out the adorable back door, I would be home in bed about now with the covers pulled over my head!"

Gaston was partly right and partly overoptimistic. When they heard a hiss from the edge of the banana plantation and veered that way to join old Julio and the others, they saw that about half the men and one or two women who'd been locked up with them had indeed lit out. But eight men and a dozen women had stayed with old Julio. As they all started talking at once, one gathered that the women, A: couldn't run as fast, and B: were so afraid of rape that some of them had to be good-looking. It was hard to tell right now.

Captain Gringo told everyone to shut up, and when they simmered down to a roar he said, "All right, muchachas y muchachos. My name is Ricardo Walker and I am called Captain Gringo. This is my compañero, Lieutenant Gaston Verrier, late of the French Foreign Legion. Nobody has paid us to fight in this dumb civil war, so we are not for either side. We are for ourselves. Does anyone here have a plan?"

No answer.

He nodded grimly and said, "So be it. We're too far from the Rio San Juan to make it to Costa Rica in one jump. I'm not sure Costa Rica would approve of all you Nicaraguans immigrating en masse in any case."

Old Julio asked, "What about Greytown, Captain Gringo?" So the tall American said, "Tell me about it. What's at Greytown and how far is it?"

The old man explained, "Greytown is perhaps thirty kilometers this side of the border. It is a British treaty base. Our various governments keep complaining to Queen Victoria about a British base on Nicaragua's coast, but what can we do about it? Tio Sam signed a treaty with Juan Toro giving Britain permission for to keep some gunboats there in exchange for a free hand to meddle in the Panamanian situation."

"Oh, yeah, I remember reading about the agreement setting aside the Monroe Doctrine as far as the Brits are concerned right now. But Gaston and me are sort of wanted by the Brits on some silly charges. I'm not sure a British enclave would welcome us with open arms."

Gaston had been listening. He said, "We most surely cannot stay here! Let us drop these unfortunates off at Greytown, where they may at least find employment washing dishes or something. Unencumbered, the two of us can make thirty kilometers and a modest river in one night, non?"

Captain Gringo nodded but didn't start running. So Gaston added, "Why are we lurking about this rough neighborhood, Dick? Those soldados will soon recover from the effects of your smoke bomb and resultant fire, non?"

"I hope so. I don't want to hang around here all night."

Gaston dropped the end of the gunbelt to stare pensively across the open field at the burning whatever, as he said, "Forgive me, I am missing something. We are many miles from Greytown or anywhere else at all good for one's health, Dick. Even had we left hours ago, the lovely tropic sunrise would have caught us on the thrice accursed open trail. It is not getting any earlier as we stand here chatting, with those très annoyed soldados doubtless forming up a posse at the moment on the far side of that old sugar mill."

Captain Gringo said, "Yeah. Get our side spread out and on the ground for cover. Two pistols and one HMG won't do for a band of twenty-three boys and girls if we mean to fight our way anywhere important."

"True, but where are we to get weapons for one and all on such short notice?" Gaston began. Then he sighed and said, "Merde alors, I might have known, you très noisy kleptomaniac! All right, my children, let us all spread out and recline upon the muck as our gallant leader suggests, hein?"

Old Julio caught on first and started helping Gaston get the bewildered runaways into position amid the banana stalks, as Captain Gringo dropped to his knees with the heavy Maxim trained out across the open field.

Gaston rejoined him as the sky to the north grew even brighter. The dapper little Frenchman observed, "The sugar mill seems to be on fire now. I forget where I left that lamp we found. Do you have any water in the jacket of that thing? What if the head spacing is set wrong? Your skills as a machine gunner are in demand down here mostly because most of the local species of soldado has no idea how to man modern automatique weaponry and . . .''

''Shut up. I just spotted a head peeking out the back of that sugar mill. That's not what's lighting up the sky. They've given up trying to put out the burning posada. So they have no place to sleep right now, and let's hope they're mad as hell about it!''

Apparently they were. As the two soldiers of fortune watched, someone across the way shouted something dumb about footprints, and a long skirmish line of soldados with rifles carried at port detached itself from the mass of the sugar mill and proceeded to cross the open field without so much as a man on point. One jerk-off was waving a tin sword as he strutted smack in the center of the line. Gaston snorted in disgust and said, ''I remember that sword. He is the species of insect who arrested us at the plaza this evening. Surely he knows by now that you left with that machine gun, non?''

''Maybe not. They have us all down as simple souls they meant to use for target practice in the cold gray light of dawn. They're just going through the motions so that when their superiors ask, they can say they tried. They think we all hit the back door running and haven't stopped since.''

''Oui, they must, from the casual way they advance across open ground. What are we waiting for, my hesitant child? They are now within range, and I grow tired of bracing myself for the chatter of that Maxim. Are you checking the action?''

Captain Gringo shook his head and said, ''Did that, first thing, as we took off. She's in shape to fire dry, for at least a belt's worth.''

''Merde alors! *Fire*, then! They are almost on top of us now!''

Captain Gringo waited another two full seconds, braced the Maxim on his hip, and said, ''When you're right you're right,'' as he squeezed the trigger.

He traversed from left to right at groin level, mowing down the skirmish line with his first traverse and then swinging the muzzle back the other way to chop up the men on the ground with his reverse traverse. He had a third of the belt left when he decided that would do for now. In the dark the muzzle of the Maxim glowed red. They did that when you fired them dry.

Neither soldier of fortune said anything as they listened in the sudden silence. Somewhere behind them that same dame was crying again. None of the soldados stretched out on the red furrows made a peep as Captain Gringo waited to see if anyone across the way had anything to say. He'd of course crabbed sideways on his knees away from the muzzle flashes, which some spoilsport in the sugar mill might have pinpointed by now.

Gaston snorted in disgust and said, "Merde alors! Such bushes of the league should not be allowed to wear uniforms. May we salvage their money and weapons and be on our way now?"

"Go ahead. I'll cover you. Make sure you get all their ammo bandoleers. If their rifles are chambered for the same .30-30s as this Maxim, we're in business. If they're not, I don't like to pack useless junk!"

Gaston whistled for old Julio and headed out across the field in a running crouch without waiting for an answer. The old man and six others had the makings of guerrillas. They ran out to join Gaston and proceeded to loot the dead. One machine-gunned soldado turned out to be still alive, albeit badly wounded. Old Julio finished him off with the bayonet of his own rifle. Yeah, old Julio had been in at least one uprising before he'd wised up and gone back to raising bananas or whatever.

It only took a few minutes for the salvagers to gather twenty-one rifles, all the ammo, and whatever the dead had in their pockets. As they headed back, Captain Gringo rose and

hoisted the now cooled Maxim to one shoulder, telling Gaston,
"Take the lead. I'll take the tail with this heavy weapon.
Hand me a couple of those bandoleers and distribute the other
guns and ammo among our people as you line 'em up and
move 'em out!"

Gaston did as he was told, with a minimum of conversation
for a change. In action, the old legionaire soldiered well.
Captain Gringo stood near the tree line, gazing fondly across
the open field at the pricks he'd gunned down, until he could
tell by the sounds behind him that it was time to go. He said,
"Adiós, motherfuckers," and followed the column of escapees into the bananas.

It was black as a bitch away from the clearing, but he
managed to keep on the natural path the planters had left
between the neatly lined-up stalks. You never knew when and
where you might need a belt of fresh ammo. So as he walked
he disengaged the partly spent canvas belt and started thumbing
.30-30s from the leather bandoleers Gaston had handed him
into the machine-gun belt. It was a good thing the local
warlord who'd ordered a machine gun had thought to specify
.30-30. Usually, these British-made toys were chambered for
British army rounds. As he emptied the first rifle bandoleer he
cast it aside. He knew he was leaving sign for future trackers,
but what the hell, the ground was soft and any greenhorn
would be able to cut their trail as soon as it was daylight.

The bananas gave out. He could see the others dimly as he
followed them across another field, still reloading his machine-
gun belt. They were outlined in ghostly green instead of ruby
now. He glanced to the east and muttered, "That was timing
it nicely. The dawn figures to come up like thunder any
minute." He called out in a louder tone, "Hey, Gaston! Wait
up. This isn't going to work!"

The others stopped and formed a clump as he moved up to
join Gaston and old Julio. He said, "Don't bunch up,

kiddies. Make it hard for guys to drop two of you with one bullet.''

As they edged back, not enough to matter, he said, ''It'll soon be light. They had a telegraph line running from that fishing village. How come we're trending in-land, Julio?''

The old man said, ''In God's truth, I have no great grasp of geography. The village lay on a bay, so naturally, if we keep going due south . . .''

''We can't,'' Captain Gringo cut in, explaining, ''As we get away from the swampy coastline we figure to run into more and more open croplands like this. We need cover, preferably where not too many people with telegraphs or telephones hang out. It's time we started thinking about making them work at trailing us, too. How bad are the mangroves due east, Julio?''

''South of the bay, señor? Nobody travels along the Mos-quito Coast to the south of the bay. It is impenetrable jungle swamp!''

Captain Gringo smiled thinly and said, ''Bueno. Gaston, take the lead. Bear south-sou'west until you find us a fox trot running east. Got the picture?''

''Oui, but I don't like it. Mosquitoes make me itch.''

''You like a bullet up the ass better?''

''Well, since you put it that way . . . Fall in, my children, Uncle Gaston shall show you the way to grandmère's house, if he does not step on a snake or crocodile first!''

They crossed that field, went through a cactus hedge, and crossed yet another field of knee-high tobacco, and it was getting almost light enough to see colors when Gaston pushed through the cactus on the far side and stopped to stare in disgust at a wide expanse of shimmering water. It was a fresh paddy of lowland rice. Gaston sat on the bank and proceeded to remove his mosquito boots as old Julio asked why, saying, ''We can easily go around that muck, no?''

Gaston said, "Oui, but at the cost of leaving footprints in the soggy soil of your adorable nation. This paddy is wide. The mud we disturb will heal itself as we flounder gaily due east through the shin-deep water. But let us hurry, my old and rare. The sun is about to pop over the treetops at us any moment and I find it très annoying to be caught in the open by the dawn's early light!"

By the time Captain Gringo caught up to push through the cactus, Gaston already had the others moving in a curving column across the paddy. The tall American nodded with approval and followed. He had too much to pack to worry about removing his boots. So the paddy mud kept trying to suck them off as he followed, trying to avoid stepping in the holes left in the soft muck. It took a million years and the sky above was pearl gray by the time they'd all gathered along the east edge of the big paddy. Gaston looked up and said, "Regardez, it looks like more rain."

Captain Gringo said, "Good. It's wet where we're going anyway and some rain would make us even tougher to track. What's on the far side of those hedges?"

"Weeds. The ground is already getting marshy to the east, and the species of mud puppies who decided to grow rice back there have run a drainage ditch through glandular grass only an elephant would wish to picnic on."

"Okay, follow the ditch until further notice."

Gaston didn't argue. Gaston was good at staying alive. But one of the other men in the improvised guerrilla band protested, "We will be eaten alive by leeches if we wade in that ditch, Captain Gringo!"

Captain Gringo swung the mass on his shoulder to face the stranger. The other escapee was a heavyset youth with a handsome face marred by a double chin and an apparently built-in pout. Captain Gringo asked, "How are you called, muchacho?" and the complainer said, "I am called Diego

Robles. Tio Julio was the brother of my father, before the damned Leónistos killed him in the last uprising.''

Another man, older and skinnier, protested, ''That is not true, Diego! I mean no disrespect, but we Leónistos had nothing to do with your late and revered father trying to hold up that bank!''

Captain Gringo handed Diego the heavy machine gun, saying, ''Here, carry this for me, and if any leeches bother you, shoot the little sons of bitches. Let's go, gang. Gaston, you're still on point.''

Gaston sat down, put his boots back on, and said, ''Merde alors, I knew I was in for wet feet.''

Diego protested, ''For why must I carry this gun, Captain Gringo? It is heavy, and it is not mine. I do not feel this is just!''

''It's a cruel world, Diego. I'll tell you what. Hand the gun to one of these girls and just go back and give yourself up if you don't want to come along with the rest of us. If you *do* want to come along, we'd best get a few points straight. I'm in command and I give the orders. I just ordered you to pack that Maxim. You ready, Gaston?''

Gaston got back up, said, ''Of course not,'' and waded into the irrigation ditch. A couple of the girls followed, bitching about leeches and the icky mud against their bare feet.

Diego stood undecided with the Maxim in his arms like a baby he didn't really feel like changing. His uncle said, ''You must make allowances for the boy, Captain Gringo. He has always been a delicate youth. He suffers from el vomito negro. Let me carry the machine gun, no?''

Captain Gringo said, ''No. I told *him* to. Nobody suffers from yellow jack on a regular basis. I've already had it. You either get better and never catch it again or it kills you. He doesn't look dead. He looks fat and lazy. Get going, viejo. Are you ready, darling Diego?''

''Sí, but I still say it is not just!''

"It's a cruel world. Get going. You there, in the red skirt, hold it and let that guy with the rifle file behind Diego. I'll follow you. How are you called, muchacha?"

The girl said, "I am called Consuela, and I am most frightened, señor!"

She had a right to be. She was maybe seventeen or eighteen and weighed about a hundred pounds soaking wet. She was pretty enough to worry about being raped, even if one didn't fancy Mestiza features set between raven's wings of long black hair in a heart-shaped face. Her Spanish blood was probably Basque. He'd never laid a Basque he hadn't thoroughly enjoyed. Come to think of it, most Indian gals screwed good too. He told her to call him Dick and slapped her on the ass to move her after the last man in the column. She gleeped and followed, lifting the hem of her skirts as the water in the ditch rose as high as her knees.

It only came part way up Captain Gringo's shins as he followed, after a last look back across the still thankfully deserted rice paddy to their rear. In no time at all they were passing through a tunnel of reedy grass that rose a good twelve feet to arch together over their heads. The ditch walk of course would leave no trail for anyone to follow. So things were looking up despite something that buzzed in Captain Gringo's ear, thirsting for his blood. He reached in his shirt and took out a purloined cigar. He lit it and called ahead, "All you guys with smokes, light up. Make the damned bugs as uncomfortable as we are!"

He heard a loud splash up ahead. He swore, eased past Consuela and the rifleman ahead of her, and confronted Diego standing empty-handed, staring down at the water between them. Diego said, "I dropped the machine gun."

Captain Gringo said, "I noticed. Don't just stand there,

you idiot. Finish lighting your damned cigar and then pick it up!''

''Is it not ruined now, Captain Gringo?''

''I hope not. But you'll be, if you try that again.''

He turned to a nearby rifleman, a small wiry peon with a lived-in face and grizzled beard. He asked, ''Are you related to this calabaza, old friend?''

The old peon shook his head and said, ''I never met any of you before. I came in from the west for to sell my charcoal, and the next thing I knew we were all locked up together. I am called Perrito. My real name is not important until I someday make it back to my own village again.''

''That sounds fair, Perrito. All right, I want you to make sure that machine gun comes along with us. Agreed?''

''Of course. I was most pleased with the way you used it on those men who meant to shoot us with it. You wish for me to carry it?''

''No. I wish for you to shoot that silly son of a bitch if he drops it again. Are you paying attention, Diego?''

The sullen youth gripped his lit cigar between his teeth and bent to pick the Maxim up from its watery grave. It was dripping mud as black as Diego's apparent mood. He said, ''I'll get my shirt dirty, damm it.''

Captain Gringo raised an eyebrow at old Perrito. The peon grinned and worked the bolt of his army rifle to load the chamber. Diego paled, hoisted the mucky Maxim to his shoulder, and started loping after Gaston and the others, sobbing and smoking at the same time.

Perrito followed. Captain Gringo said, ''Okay, Consuela, move your pretty posteriora. You can't see it down here in the weeds, but it must be broad daylight now. What are you waiting for, a streetcar?''

''Forgive me, I know it is rude, but I have been thinking, Deek.''

"You're right. Pretty little girls should never think at times like these. But, okay, let's hear it, Consuela."

"By now they are no longer serious about shooting us all, no?"

"By now, if any of them are left, they ought to be serious, yes. Let me finish for you. You were thinking about making a solo break for your own village or whatever, right?"

"Sí, if I were to make my way to my own village, while I still have at least a hazy idea where it is . . ."

"Maybe," he cut in, asking, "How far is it from the plaza we were all swept in off, Consuela?"

She thought and said, "Three or four kilometers. Why?"

"Keep walking. Those soldados figure to shoot all the pigs and chickens for miles around the last place we met up with 'em. Before you say something dumb about warning your own people, forget it. Any peones who haven't heard about the sweep and its unexpected outcome are as good as dead. If they listen good to machine-gun fire in the distance, your villagers are headed somewhere else, too, right now. Your best bet is to stick with us."

She started wading on ahead of him, but asked over her shoulder if he had any idea where they were going. He shook his head and said, "Not for the next few hours. If we last through the day, we may make that run for Greytown. We may not. You take one day at a time in times like these, muchacha. Hello, everyone seems to have stopped up ahead. Stay here and let me see what Gaston's tripped over."

He made his way up the column, reassuring one and all and getting a better look at them now that it was daylight. A couple of the men looked tough, and more than one of the girls was as good-looking as Consuela. He made a mental note to leave his options open by refraining from those friendly pats on Consuela's ass, for now.

He found Gaston staring pensively up at a tree. A big one.

Standing in water the color of tea and not much cooler. The tree was not alone. Gaston said, "As you can see, the ditch ends in this lovely cypress swamp. The Caribbean is saline, ergo there is some dry ground between here and the coastal mangroves. Do we go right, left, or forge ahead?"

Captain Gringo thought and said, "Left takes us back to the bay and that occupied fishing village. Dead ahead probably means a sandy rise that could lead soldados down the coast for a modest patrol. Okay, let's head south."

"Through all this water, Dick?"

"What's the matter, are you afraid of getting your feet wet? We need some soggy miles between us and those soldados before we even stop to piss. Move it out. If we find a dry hammock by noon we can stop for a siesta. But don't stop this side of noon."

It was more like one in the afternoon before Gaston staggered onto an island in the vast cypress swamp. The overhead forest canopy kept the hammock fairly free of undergrowth, so it would have been dry, if it hadn't started to rain. As the escapees threw themselves down, exhausted, on the already damp sand, Captain Gringo peered up at a cielito of sky showing through the canopy and said, "Smoke shouldn't show against that overcast, and we're all going to catch pneumonia if we don't dry off once in a while."

He turned to Tio Julio and said, "Julio, detail some men to build lean-tos and fires, pronto. I don't want one big fire. I want half-a-dozen small ones, with lean-tos facing them. Get the picture?"

"Sí, my captain. Widely spaced small fires do not send up a big pillar of smoke for nosy people on rooftops to gaze upon, eh?"

"You're learning. I think we ought to be over the horizon

from that village we escaped from, but why take chances? Spread our people out across this sand. Make the bastards work at shooting us up if I guessed wrong about the footprints we didn't leave.''

As the old man went on duty, shouting orders with obvious relish, the tall American found sulky Diego seated on a fallen palmetto with the Maxim leaning against it, firing action half-buried in the sand. Captain Gringo swore and told the idiot to go jerk off in the bushes or something as he took Diego's place on the log. He picked up the machine gun and held it across his knees to survey the damage. Then he swore some more. The Maxim was covered with half-dry crud. He knew if worked the bolt he figured to scratch the metal with any sand it had inhaled due to Diego's latest and probably deliberate stupidity.

The soft rain splashing down on the abused weapon was helping to gently wash some of the muck away. Gaston came over to ask how bad it was. Captain Gringo said, ''Bad. Can I borrow that pig sticker of yours?''

''But of course. Who do you wish to stab, Dick?''

''Diego. But his uncle might not like it, and old Julio may come in handy as a guide. I need a screwdriver more than I need your snicker snee, but somehow I can't seem to find a tool shop open around here.''

Gaston nodded and drew his collar knife, saying as he handed it over, ''Be careful with that tip, Dick. Stabbing with a dull knife is très fatigué.''

Captain Gringo nodded and gingerly unscrewed the feed plate to ease out the wet, swollen, canvas ammo belt. He handed it to Gaston, saying, ''So far so good. Find a place to hang this up to dry, will you? Not by a fire, by the way!''

''Merde alors, I was drying wet ammo when your mother was changing your wet diapers, my child. I don't think fresh water will have corroded the primers on such nicely greased rounds. If the idiot had dropped them in *salt* water, ooh la la!''

Gaston wandered off, talking to the long ammo belt, as Captain Gringo dropped a screw in the sand, cursed, stuck the knife in the log, and gingerly got the screw back before it could sink out of sight.

Consuela came over to join him, saying, ''I told the old one I meant to share the lean-to and fire they just built for us, Deek. Is there anything else I can do for you?''

''Yeah, take off that skirt and spread it on the sand.''

''Are you serious?''

''I sure am. I have to field strip this weapon and there's nothing like a workbench in sight. Come on, muchacha muñeca. That red circle skirt is perfect to see small parts against, and what the hell, you're wearing a blouse.''

''Sí, but this blouse does not come to my knees under the skirts, and, ah, I am not wearing pantalones!''

''So what? I've already seen your knees, and all the others are holed up out of the rain and out of sight from here. Come on, Consuela. We're both getting wet, and the sooner I clean this machine gun, the sooner we can join them around the fires!''

The pert Mestiza hesitated, giggled, and unfastened her skirt to spread it on the sand as she ducked down on the far side of the log from the others. Captain Gringo didn't comment on the fact that she'd overstated the length of her blouse tails as he joined her on his knees with the gun on the circle of red cotton. She was holding the lower hem of her blouse as far down her lap as she could. So, had he been on her far side, her little brown behind would have been well exposed. But that wasn't the reason he'd asked for the loan of her skirt.

It wasn't so bad, once he started taking the Maxim apart and spreading the parts on the cotton. He didn't wipe anything. The gun had been well oiled by its previous owner. So the rain stood in beads on the oily steel and ran off with the muck and grains of sand with little help, now that the rain could get at it. Consuela complained that her skirt was getting dirty. He nodded and said, "Better that than a machine gun that won't shoot when you want it to. We'll rinse the cloth out in the swamp water, after. You may have some grease spots, when and if it ever dries out again. But consider the alternatives."

She did, and said with a shudder, "I was so afraid those soldados would, you know, before they shot us. Don't you think it curious that they did not molest any of us girls back there, Deek?"

"I suppose they had their own adelitas in the posada across the way. But you make a good point, Consuela. Those guys had orders to massacre any and all strangers. They would have raped and slapped people around more if they'd just been letting off the usual steam. Do you remember spotting any military secrets before they rounded you up with the rest of us?"

She looked blank and said, "Military secrets? I came into town with a load of peppers for to sell at the market. After I sold them for my papa; I thought I would, you know, stroll about the plaza a few times to see what life was like in the big city."

"Yeah, I know how the paseo works. Had things gone different, we may well have met that way instead of this. I don't even know which side those bastards were on, do you?"

"No. Both sides wear those same khaki uniforms, unless they are irregulars, of course. Some of the men locked up with us last night say they are for the Léon cause, while others favor Granada. I am only a woman, so I do not know which cause is the right one, do you?"

"No, I'm only a man, and I've never been able to see much difference between guys who shoot the pigs and then the chickens or guys who shoot the chickens and then the pigs. I should think you little people down here would be pretty sick of both sides by now.''

"Oh, we are. My papa says we are all to run and hide no matter who comes by in uniform on horseback. Some of the older men say things were better when the conservatives of Granada were running things. Others say it is better to have the liberal party of León in charge. What is the difference between a conservative and a liberal, Deek?''

"Down here? Not much. As I gathered from my last visit, Spain left two Creole cliques behind when they pulled out back in the twenties. Spain never said who was in charge. Everyone in Nicaragua was shooting at them as they got in the boats. Once they got the Spanish off their necks, the Grenada and León colonies sized up the situation, reloaded their guns, and they've been fighting each other ever since.''

"That is what my papa says. Do you know who is supposed to be running the country at the moment, Deek? We pay taxes mostly to Granada.''

"That figures. We're closer, here, to Granada. Washington has recognized the government in León. Someone running steamboats on the lakes told Uncle Sam that León offered the more stable government.''

He held the operating rod up to the light, saw it looked okay, and put it aside, muttering, ''A stable is where you find horse shit.''

"Es verdad. For why does Tio Sam in Washington feel so free to choose governments down here, Deek? We are not allowed for to vote in your Yanqui elections, you know.''

"I've noticed that, doll face. Don't try to understand Manifest Destiny, Consuela. I spent four years at West Point and I'm damned if I can understand it either. Neither of us are in the steamboat or banana business. So Washington would hardly want to hear *our* opinions on the current political situation in Nicaragua."

He started putting parts back together as the rain washed them free of grit. He knew he needed gun oil, fast, but hopefully nothing would rust solid for a day or so, thanks to the oil already in situ. Consuela asked pensively when he thought there would be peace at last in Nicaragua. He balanced the Maxim on the log, saying, "That ought to hold it," and added, "Peace in our time is a dream to hang on to, kid. But meanwhile, keep your powder dry. That ain't easy, in this climate."

She started to cry, saying, "Oh, I wish everyone would go away and leave us alone. If nobody sold guns and bullets to the warring factions, my papa says the little people would be able for to make peace with their machetes."

"Papa sounds like a kindly old philosopher, honey. Hey, what's with the tears? We've got guns and a good head start on whoever those troopers were working for. If our luck holds out, you'll be safe in Greytown in a day or so. What do you want, egg in your cerveza?"

She went on crying, leaning his way. So he found it only natural to take her in his arms and comfort her. He had no idea how they wound up flat atop her skirt in the sand, with him on top and the rain coming down on his back as he kissed her.

Consuela kissed back, with more enthusiasm and skill than expected from a simple country girl. She'd said she'd been arrested at the paseo. He doubted very much that it had been the first one she'd ever attended.

When they came up for air, she giggled at the raindrop that hit her in one big brown eye and said, "We are getting very wet. Would not this be more comfortable over under the lean-to, with the fire?"

He replied, "I don't know. Is the lean-to in plain view of any others?"

She giggled again and said, "Sí, but what of it?—unless we wish for to be very naughty. Do we wish for to be very naughty, Deek?"

That was a dumb question, considering that her blouse hem was up around her waist now, and her unspoken reply to his exploratory hand was to spread her brown thighs wider. So he kissed her again to stem the pointless conversation as he unbuckled and unbuttoned his pants for action. This forced him to forgo his advantage with her naked lap for a moment, so of course she started muttering things about not being that kind of a girl, until he was in her, and she was.

Consuela braced her bare heels in the sand at either side and began to bump and grind enthusiastically in time with his thrusts as she insisted she was at least close to being still a virgin and asked if he was sure nobody was peeking. He assured her nobody was likely to come out in all this rain, and it was in fact starting to rain like hell on his bare ass and already soaked-through shirt as he bounced in the soft warm saddle of her welcoming thighs. He started peeling off his shirt. Consuela protested, "It is broad daylight. Are you without any shame at all?"

He said, "No, I'm wet. Nobody's going to laugh any harder at my bare back than anything else bounding in the wind and rain, doll. We'd better get you out of that wet blouse, too. Wet cloth feels clammier on the skin than plain old water."

She gasped, "Oh, no, I couldn't," as she helped him pull the damp cotton up between them and off over her head. As they snuggled naked together at last she sighed and said, "Oh, it does feel ever so much cozier this way. But if someone should come . . . Oh, Jesus, Maria, y José! I think I *am*!"

That made two of them. He hadn't had any sex since escaping from Honduras with Gaston, and Gaston wasn't that kind of a boy. A few hours before, he'd expected to die without ever getting laid again. It had done wonders for his appetite, although, in truth, Consuela was so good he could have managed in any case. She must have needed it too, for she didn't ask questions when he kept on going after they'd come together. She just closed her eyes against the rain dripping from his hair and moved like love poetry until they'd climaxed together a second time. As he went limp in her arms she sighed and said, "Oh, that was so lovely, toro mio! Do we not fit together hand in glove?"

It felt more to him like thumb in a mighty tight whatever. But as cool as it was with the rain pattering down through the leaves onto them, he needed to catch his second wind, so he kissed her and rolled off to lie semisated on his back, with the rain washing off his old organ grinder. Consuela took it as an invitation to get on top. So she did. She squatted above him with her heels firmly planted on either side of his bare hips, as she braced her palms on his chest with her wet brown breasts hugged between the upper arms. She lowered herself onto his erection with a contented moan, saying, "Oh, it feels bigger this way. You are right about the others. I can see nobody else, even from up here!"

He admired the view, though, as she started bouncing all over. He didn't want her poor flopping boobs to bruise themselves, so he reached up and cupped one in each palm to save them from harm. She laughed down at him and leaned forward to press the nipples between his rain-wet fingers, asking if he liked her all over. She sure talked childishly for such an obviously experienced sex maniac. But he knew women were like that, so he told her she suited him just fine from the part of her hair to the part he was parting with his reinspired tool.

She asked, "Am I to be your one and only adelita, Deek?" as she poised on the upstroke, taking unfair advantage of a man on the razor's edge of coming. He said, "Sure, sure, I'll go home with you to meet your folks. But for God's sake don't stop now!''

"My legs are starting to cramp, soldado mio!''

"Okay, okay already! Let me get on top to finish!''

She rolled off, to land face down on the red cotton as he rolled over and above her. He didn't roll her on her back. He parted the wet cheeks of her pretty little brown rump and threw the blocks to her dog-style as she giggled and said he was making her feel very naughty. Then she arched her spine and started chewing on the hem of her skirt as she bit down hard on his shaft with her internal muscles and took all he had to offer, then milked the last drops from his thoroughly detonated weapon.

She sighed as he withdrew and suggested another position calculated to shock passersby indeed. He said, "I know we're nice and clean from all this rain, but I really would feel silly going sixty-nine in broad ass daylight. If we don't rejoin the others, someone's bound to wander over to see if we've been eaten by alligators, querida.''

"Pooh, I saw you first. Let the alligators eat each other. Just once, to see what you taste like, soldado mio? A good adelita must pleasure her soldado in every way, no?''

"Me and my big mouth! Okay, we'll do all sorts of wild and woolly things later. Right now we'd better join the others and get halfway dry. I have to dry that machine gun off for sure, and it's raining fire and salt now.''

They dressed and found the camp. The lean-to Consuela had reserved for them was nice and dry under the overhang, with the fire burning in front hard enough to sizzle the falling rain. He placed the wet Maxim on the palmetto-leaf floor and sat down facing the fire to get his bearings as Consuela settled beside him, hooking a possessive arm through his.

On the far side of the fire, Gaston was staring at them from under his own improvised shelter, wearing a bemused and worldly smile. Gaston had strung the ammo belt up to dry.

He'd also apparently suggested one of the other girls share his lean-to with him. She looked bemused, too. She was dropdead beautiful, damn Gaston for a son of a bitch who could wait!

Gaston nodded and waved. The vision beside him just went on staring, either at them or the fire between them and Gaston's lean-to. She was a little older and a lot more filled out than the somewhat skinny albeit big-chested Consuela. Her features were more Hispanic. Her hair was a dusky shade of auburn. All over. She sat with her knees drawn up, resting her elbows on them. Her peon skirt didn't do the job it was doubtless meant to. Consuela giggled and called across, "Oh, Rubia, you are, ah, exposing your private parts to us!"

The redhead called Rubia, if that was her name and not just a nickname that fit her hair all over, put her legs closer together, which helped a little, and replied to Consuela's giggles with a bored expression. Consuela whispered to Captain Gringo, "She is used to being the most popular girl at el paseo. I do not think she finds your older friend her type."

Captain Gringo muttered, "That's not our problem, doll box." Then, in a louder voice and in English, he called across, "How's it going, Gaston?"

Gaston called back, "I don't think she has an Electra complex, alas. I would ask you how you made out, but I can tell time without a watch. What do we do now? We've no food. We're surrounded by miles of this same très fatigué cypress swamp, according to Tio Julio, and I fear it will rain harder before it lets up."

Captain Gringo nodded and switched to Spanish so the others could follow the loud conversation when he called back, "We may as well stay put until the rain stops. We wouldn't want to be caught by nightfall soaked to the skin in knee-deep water. In fact, since nobody could possibly be on our trail right now, we may as well just hole up here snug and dry for the rest of the day and the night. We'll get a fresh start in the morning, dry and rested.''

From the grunts and mutterings in the other lean-tos more or less in sight, it seemed most of the others had no better plan. But pouty Diego stuck his head out down the line to bawl, ''We have nothing for to eat! By the beard of Christ, how long do you expect a man to go without food?''

Captain Gringo called back, ''A *man* can go a week or so without food, easy, as long as he has water. Look around you if you're thirsty, kid.''

''Madre de Dios! I have never gone a full day without something for to eat, Captain Gringo!''

''I believe you. None of us are going to enjoy being on a diet, Diego. But staying alive is more important than stuffing your gut. The rule is four, four, forty. A healthy adult can go four minutes without air, four days without water, and forty days without food. None of us should feel weak until we've fasted a good seventy-two hours or more, and I didn't say we'd camp here quite that long.''

Tio Julio called out, ''May I make a suggestion, Captain Gringo? There is edible mangrove fruit not far to the east, nearer salt water. One could easily get over there and back before dark, no?''

''No. If I wanted to advertise where we were holed up, I'd have left a paper trail, viejo. Anyone looking for us could be smart enough to figure we'd make for more sensible parts where there's food as well as dry ground to walk on. We'll stay here for now and let them run in circles for a while. Meanwhile, we'll take advantage of this unmapped hammock to dry out and rest up. I don't want any further argument about it, muchachas y muchachos. I suggest if none of you thought to bring along a good book, you can just reflect on how much nicer it is out here in this swamp than it was in that cellar last night. Gaston and I didn't *have* to bring you people along. If you want to stay with us, you do things our way.''

A dark, hatchet-faced man Captain Gringo didn't have a name to go with yet stepped out in the rain to call out. "What if we split up and each went our own way, now that we have guns and a good head start, captain?"

"What's your name, amigo?"

"I am called Hachismo. I mean no harm to anyone here. But I am of the León party. Like the rest of you, I was arrested for no reason by those soldados. I think they were not real soldados. When I told them I was for the government, they hit me and took my money anyway."

Captain Gringo nodded and said, "We're all in this together until further notice. Nobody leaves on their own. It's too late. I don't care if someone wants to commit suicide by trying to dodge an army on his or her own. But I do mind them answering questions. You all know where we are and the general direction we're going. You're getting all wet, Hachismo. Like I said, I don't want to talk about it anymore."

The ugly man with the oddly apt nickname ducked out of sight, muttering. In English, Gaston observed, "You know, of course, that after dark we may have difficulty keeping our little flock together, my tedious Good Shepherd?"

Captain Gringo nodded and said, "Meanwhile, we've the rest of the afternoon to not get shot in, and how far can any sissy stumble through a swamp in the dark?"

"Oui. On the other hand, if just you and I, with perhaps these most attractive young ladies . . ."

"Forget it. Aside from the usual bellyachers, these poor slobs are depending on us. In the old Tenth Cav we never left any of our people behind for the Apache."

"Oui, we shot wounded and stragglers in the Legion, too. But this is not a formal military establishment, and, in all fairness, I feel it is not quite fair to call those mysterious troopers we escaped from Apache, hein?"

Captain Gringo lit another smoke and shook out the match before he said, "When you're right you're right, Gaston. I had no call to insult the Apache by comparing 'em to those motherfucking sons of bitches on our trail. Apache usually have a *reason* when they kill somebody.''

The day dragged on with half the camp bitching about being hungry. The only bright spot was that the rain tapered off in the late afternoon. Captain Gringo told everyone to build the fires up and dry things out for sure before nightfall, when it came time to douse all fires for reasons even spanking-new guerrillas could grasp.

That about summed up the military skills of most of the band. When it dried off enough for Captain Gringo to call them all together for a bull session, it developed that Tio Julio had done a teen-aged hitch in the army, once, when the Granada facton was in power. Perrito and the sinister-looking Hachismo were probably part-time ladrónes who seemed to know how to hold their rifles, at least. None of the other men and of course none of the women claimed any soldiering skills, though young Diego boasted he was a crack shot and a mighty hunter. Tio Julio confirmed he held no other steady job.

All the men and half the women said they'd at least fired a gun once or twice in their lives. Gaston suggested some hasty target practice. But Captain Gringo shook his head and said, ''Not until we know who's hunting frog legs or us within the sound of rifle fire. If you feel like training troops, I suppose some dry firing should at least give everyone the feel of those bolt-action rifles.''

A sad little man asked, ''Even if we learn how to load and cock these military rifles, señor. How can we be sure of hitting anything when the time comes?''

Gaston snorted in disgust and said, ''The bullets come out the end you point away from you. If one fires a rifle in the general direction of someone else, at least they generally duck. That may be some improvement in the situation. So regardez, you grotesque excuses for an army on the march, I, Gaston, shall take you in groups of three until we at least know how to keep from shooting one another, hein?''

Captain Gringo left that detail to Gaston. He went back to his lean-to and field stripped the Maxim again, wiping the parts on his now dry shirttail before putting it back together and inserting the now dry belt. The canvas was stiff and a bit worn. The usual idea was to discard a used-up belt, not to reload it. But it looked okay.

Consuela had been watching adoringly. But the redhead, Rubia, came over to say, ''Consuela, Gaston wished for to teach you how to shoot your rifle now.''

Consuela shrugged and picked up her purloined army rifle, saying as she left, in a rather smug tone, ''I must go and learn how to shoot for my soldado. I am the adelita of this one, by the way. So do not get ideas.''

As she flounced off for her dry-firing lesson, Rubia sat down by Captain Gringo, pouting, and raised her knees again as she asked, ''Is it true you have already proposed to that little half-breed, handsome?''

He locked the Maxim on safe and stowed it out of the way in the back of the lean-to before he said, ''Proposing may be too strong a word. She seems to think we're good friends. How are you getting along with Gaston?''

Rubia raised her knees higher, in case he'd missed her being a redhead all over, and said, ''He is old enough for to be my grandfather. For why did you make Consuela your adelita? Do you find me ugly?''

''Not at all, Rubia. But first come first come, and what the hell, it's not as if there aren't any other men in this party. Old Diego's not a bad-looking muchacho, you know.''

''Bah, muchacho is all he is. It takes an *hombre* to please a real woman. What is it you like about Consuela? She is not as pretty as I am.''

"That's true, but I'm wondering if she's not a bit nicer. Look, red, I know this must come as a surprise to you, but right now I'm more worried about living than kissing. I don't want any jealousy on the trail. We have enough to worry about. Don't you agree?''

"Sí, I agree that you and I are the prettiest people here. Tell little Consuela she can be the adelita of your old French friend and that way everyone will be happy, no?''

He shook his head with a laugh and got to his feet to get away from the view up her skirts as well as to check out the perimeter of the sandy hammock they were stuck on.

She got up to follow him. He shook his head sternly and said, "Stay here. That's an order. I don't want you and Consuela fighting over me.''

"Pooh, if she wants to fight me, I can whip her as well as any other girl in our gang!''

"I thought you looked pretty tough. I don't want you fighting with anyone. If you do, I'll lick the winner. We've got all the enemies we need right now, Rubia. Fighting among ourselves would be suicidal.''

He turned and walked away, armed only with his stolen six-gun, and when he bulled through some rough brush she didn't follow. He noticed the underbrush grew thicker near the water's edge in most places. The edge was always a no-tree's-land in these parts. The reason the rivers were lined with what looked like solid walls of spinach gone crazy was that real trees tended to grow with their roots either in or out of water. The hammock was too well drained for swamp cypress. So the tall timber shading it was wild rubber and mahogany. The sand underfoot was already drying out nicely as the big thirsty dry-land trees drank the rain from the porous sand.

His circle wasn't big. The hammock was too small. He

made sure nobody was moving in on them from any direction and went to see how Gaston was doing. Gaston said he was doing lousy, but that everyone seemed at least able to load and more or less fire the rifles they'd salvaged. He held his own up and added, "I see they're Krags. U.S. Army and Marine issue, non?"

Captain Gringo shrugged and said, "They're made in Scandanavia, cheap. Uncle Sam's not the only guy who's been buying Krags lately. They're really just a rugged Chinese Copy of the more expensive Martini or Mauser."

"True, but my point is that those cochons we took them from last night are equipped with the latest in military weapons. That Maxim looks new. Like the Krags, it was chambered for easily obtained American ammunition. That means it was all ordered in advance."

"Sure. So?"

"So who in the devil were those troopers fighting for? Our Granada-faction followers don't think they could have been on their side. Our Leónistos were as unpleasantly surprised to be arrested by them. Who could be left?"

Captain Gringo said, "Try it this way. That fishing village could have been strategically important to either side. It's a natural place to run in a schooner load of guns. The high command on either side might have made a deal they don't want anyone else to know about. Both John Bull and Uncle Sam are monitoring things down here, with a view to restoring law and order. Or at least enough law and order for the business-as-usual international firms. Nobody's making any money with half the potential customers in Nicaragua trying to blow away the other half."

Gaston shrugged and said, "I read it as a warlord going into business for himself. You are right about both the usual sides down here being exhausted by an even struggle. But a new man on a white horse can always be found to, ah, save the country."

"Maybe. Those guys were uniformed and equipped pretty good for pisspot guerrillas, though."

"Merde alors, they may have been pretty, but they showed no grasp of basic infantry tactics in that open field last night. Our warlord may have some financial backing, non?"

"Could be. Someone's always fishing in troubled waters. A new dictator means a new cutting of the cards for all the kids playing for bananas, chewing gum, and steamboat franchises. Let's not worry about what those pricks wanted with a private fishing village. We're not going back. I want *out* of this dumb country poco tiempo!"

He glanced up at the tree canopy and added, "It'll be getting dark in a while. We'll let the fires go out naturally and maybe get a little heat from the coals if it doesn't rain again tonight. We'd better think about posting a perimeter guard. One picket guarding north, south, east, and west ought to do it. Nobody can creep up on us without going splashy splashy. What do you think, two hours on and four hours off?"

Gaston shook his head and said, "Even if we had a watch, formal guard mount may be too much for their peon minds to grasp. I'll chase them out on guard and relieve them when I catch them dozing off. I doubt if any can be depended on to stand watch more than an hour at a time."

Captain Gringo nodded and said, "Okay, you take the first tour as corporal of the guard and wake me up when you get bored. Unless you'd rather do it the other way?"

"Merde alors, I'll take the first watch. I don't have anyone to lay in my lean-to. By midnight I should have walked off my frustration, non?"

Captain Gringo chuckled and said, "Don't give up so easy. I was just talking to the redhead. I think you'd win if you really wanted to wrestle her for two out of three falls."

Gaston looked disgusted and said, "Eh bien, but why should I do the spoiled brat such a favor?"

"She's not bad-looking, Gaston."

"True. But not half as beautiful as she thinks she is. Nobody could be. Take it from a dirty old man, Dick. Spoiled beauties are never worth the trouble they put a man through. All cats are gray in the dark, but the ones who scratch and spit are très fatigué!"

The younger soldier of fortune agreed that Gaston had a point. He left the little Frenchman to his own devices in setting up the posts for the night and headed back to his own lean-to. As he passed the one Diego shared with his uncle, Diego called out, "I am starving!"

Captain Gringo told him he'd be hungrier before morning, but added, not unkindly, "It's like having to take a crap, Diego. The feeling tends to fade away if you don't dwell on it. Drink some water and smoke all you like. If that doesn't work, think of what the mud of a grave would taste like and remind yourself that as long as you're still alive, you can hope to eat again someday."

"Oh, my God!" sighed Diego, as the tall American walked on.

He rejoined Consuela under the lean-to. It was dry to the point of dusty now, and the swamp was heating up pretty good in the late afternoon rays of what was still a tropic sun. Consuela said it was too hot now to make love. He sat down beside her, lit another smoke, and told her to have patience, adding, "It'll be colder than a banker's heart before midnight, and we don't have any blankets."

"Ah, but we have each other, no?"

He laughed, made sure Rubia wasn't watching from across the still smoldering fire, and patted Consuela fondly, saying, "That's for sure. I wonder why that fucking sun is still staying up there like that, the no good little basser!"

She said she could hardly wait for darkness, too. So a

million years went by as they sat there holding hands and watching the shadows deepen by imperceptible shades. He went to the water's edge to fetch them a pail of water, or at least some water in an improvised cup of leaves bound with palmetto string. He took a leak as long as he was at it. He wondered why he had a hard-on, considering. He didn't worry about it. He sure wouldn't be able to read in bed tonight.

He was laughing to himself about that when he rejoined the little Mestiza. Consuela asked what was so funny, and he said, "Life. When a guy has time to kill with a good book, he always wishes he had something softer in bed with him. Someday, in a lonely hotel room, I figure to remember this night fondly. But, shit, I'm not used to starting at six, and that's when the sun goes down in the tropics!"

"Do not you wish for to make love to me anymore?"

"Sure I do. But we have a whole dull night to kill. Let's try and hold out until at least nine or so, huh?"

They didn't. The sun sank slower than a cat shitting through a tin funnel for what seemed like hours and hours, and then, as was its custom in the tropics, the sun went out without so much as a warning blink.

He said, "Sky above the trees must be clear again." But Consuela wasn't listening. She was already clutching at his pants in the sudden darkness she'd been waiting for.

He saw that the fire out front was dead. He couldn't see across to Rubia, so obviously she couldn't see what Consuela was doing. It was just as well. Consuela had his erection out and was sucking hell out of him in the dark. He started to object that he wanted to finish undressing and do it right. But what the hell, he was a little tired, very erect, and the poor kid hadn't had any supper.

Apparently that was what she'd had in mind. Because after he'd fired a round into her bobbing head she swallowed with a moan of pleasure, sighed, and said, "Oh, God, that tasted good going down! Would you like to go down on me, Deek?''

He thought and said, "Not really. I don't like to nibble herring hors d'oeuvres unless I mean to sit down to a full meal. Tasting anything yummy would just be torturing my rumbling tummy."

So they finished stripping and he got aboard to do it right, if old-fashioned. As he entered her once more Consuela moaned, "Oh, yes, shove it to me all the way, toro mio!"

He whispered, "I am, damn it! But keep it down to a roar. I don't want anyone else to hear us and we're right in camp."

She locked her brown legs around his naked waist and answered, "I don't care if anyone knows we are fucking. I want them all to know I am your adelita forever!"

"Hush, let them figure some things out for themselves. Do you want to make love or do you just want to show off, Consuela?"

"Both!" she announced to the world in general, adding, "Oh, this is marvelous! I can feel you hitting bottom with every stroke and I love the way your ostras bounce in the estria de me abajo! Faster, caballero! Ride me hard and make me—oooooooooh!"

Someone across the way got up and flounced away, kicking sand and hissing like a frustrated steam boiler as the somewhat annoyed Captain Gringo faked an orgasm and relaxed aboard Consuela, saying, "You can cut the dramatics now. I think she got the message that somebody was getting something *she* wasn't getting around here."

Consuela laughed and said, "Bueno. It serves her right for being so stuck up. Do you think I am as pretty as Rubia, Deek?"

"Oh, sure," he lied, adding, "There's no comparison."

She held him closer and said, "I am glad you think I am pretty. Do you wish for me to suck you some more?"

"No, thanks. If you're getting tired, why not try sleep as a new thrill. You haven't had any since about this time twenty-four hours ago, remember?"

"I am not sleepy. Maybe a little," she protested, as he lay in her arms, and in her, not moving. He was at that take-it-or-leave-it stage where it wouldn't kill him to stop or come again. As he moved gently and experimentally, he noticed she was snoring softly. He muttered, "Right. Save some for a midnight snack," and gently withdrew and rolled off her. He pulled her skirt over her as the only thing in the way of a blanket available. Then he pulled on his pants, strapped on the gun rig, and crawled clear to rise and see how Gaston was doing.

He didn't find Gaston on the first try. As he eased across the hammock in his bare feet, shirtless, the moon was filtering down through the overhead canopy just enough to make out where he was going. Something he'd taken at first for another tree murmured, "Well, toro mio, a 'onde va? Haven't you had enough yet?"

Yeah, it was Rubia. The redhead detached herself from the tree bole she'd been leaning against and moved in for the kill with no preliminaries. She simply reached up to wrap her arms around his neck, thrust her pubic bone hard against his, and planted a big hungry kiss full on his lips as, not wanting to look like a sissy, he kissed her back and felt himself rising to the occasion against her hyperactive pelvis.

She laughed as she drew her lips back just enough to speak, or rather purr, as she said, "Well, I feel there is more to you than meets the eye. I knew that little bitch was just putting on an act for my ears in the dark. You never really did it, did you?"

"A gentleman never discusses such matters, Rubia. What do you think?"

She stood on her toes to rub her out-thrust pubis thought-fully over the bulge that had started to come between them and said huskily, "I know damn well you haven't had a woman in some time. Is there some place we could lie down and discuss your upbringing, you poor thing? I fear that little puta has been teasing us both shamelessly."

He laughed and said, "You'd know I was a liar if I tried to tell you I wasn't interested, Rubia. But do you always come on this strong?"

"Only when a man interests me. Would you have me play the blushing virgin with you, Deek?"

"No. That way *I'd* wind up doing the laughing. But let's get a few things straight here."

She reached down between them with one hand to grab him and squeeze him through his thin tropic pants, saying, "I'd say this thing was about as straight as it can get, Deek. My heavens, is all that just for little me?"

He sighed and muttered, "Lord, give me strength." And then, since the Lord didn't answer, he picked her up and carried her into the first clump of bushes he could find in the moonlight.

He found a little clearing and lowered the redhead to the silvery sand. Then he rolled her over on her hands and knees and threw her skirt up around her waist to expose her bare derriere as he dropped to his knees behind her and unbuttoned his fly. Rubia gasped in surprise and said, "This hardly seems romantic, and that belt buckle is cold, but, oh, well . . ."

Then she felt where he was trying to shove it and shook her head stubbornly, protesting, "Not *that* way, you idiot! I'm Nicaraguan, not Greek!"

He made his voice deliberately brutal as he asked, "What's the problem? I thought you said you fucked better than Consuela, red."

"Jesus, Maria, y José! I wished for to make love, not to be treated as a cabin boy! Don't you know how to make love to a *woman*, you brute?"

"I haven't had any complaints from my regular adelita.

Listen, maybe if you took it in your mouth to make it wet it would slide in easier.''

She fell forward on the sand, pulling her skirt down and crossing her legs as she stammered, ''Wait a moment, Deek! Maybe we should talk about this first!''

He remained kneeling over her, waving his dong at her as he asked in a happy-go-lucky tone, ''What's to talk about? You said you could top old Consuela and I believed you. Look how hard it is, red!''

''Jesus, don't come on my skirt! Listen, handsome, I can top any woman, but not with my bottom. Will you put that thing away? I've been thinking.''

''Hey, that's a dangerous thing for a woman to try. If God had wanted women to think, he'd have never built them that way. It's a simple fact of nature that ovaries and a brain can't function in the same body!''

''Oh, my god, you're one of *those*, too? Listen, Deek, little Consuela is a good friend of mine, and maybe we shouldn't be doing anything behind her back, eh?''

''Oh, hell, she won't mind. She's asleep right now. She says since she met me she needs more rest than usual.''

''I believe that! But believe me, you're all hers! I could never steal the hombre of a sweet little friend like Consuela. It would not be right.''

''Well, if you say so. But what am I to do with this inspired erection?''

She said she was sure he'd work something out, as she crawled out of range, leaped to her feet, and took off running.

He chuckled, tucked his frustrated shaft back where it couldn't get in trouble, and rose to move on. He knew his pecker hated him for what he'd just done to it. But somebody had to think straight around here, and it was unpleasant to watch two dames rolling around on the ground spitting and pulling each other's hair.

He found Gaston sitting on a log in the moonlight. As he sat down beside him, the Frenchman said, "I was just about to come looking for you."

"I'm glad you didn't. What's up?"

"That species of fat boy, Diego. I left him here on guard. As you see, he is not here. Unless he rises from the swamp like Venus from the waves, and très shortly, one must conclude he has deserted, non?"

Captain Gringo sighed and said, "Well, we didn't make him sign any articles of war, so desertion may be too strong a term. We're probably well rid of him. Did he take his uncle with him?"

"Mais non, old Julio has finished his turn on the south post and now sleeps the sleep of the just. He keeps telling me his nephew is delicate. Sacrebleu! I shall delicate him indeed the next time I see him!"

Captain Gingo said, "We probably won't. If he doesn't drown himself out there in the swamp, he'll never be able to find this place again if he's wandered far enough to matter. Why don't you turn in for forty? I'll sit here and mind the store. Maybe Diego just went hunting frogs."

"Merde alors, how could he catch a frog? Any frog has to have more intelligence than him. I'll stay and watch the fun if and when he staggers back."

"Go hit the sack. I'm not going to do anything to the asshole worth waiting up for. Now that we know for sure he's unreliable, we can just use him as a beast of burden some more. His uncle is in thick with some of the others, and if hitting Diego worked, someone would have beaten some sense into him by now."

Gaston shrugged and said, "You go back to bed, or what's in it, then. I am not at all sleepy, and as you know, I have not worked out who my adelita is to be."

Captain Gringo lit another smoke and said, "Try the redhead. I think she's out to advance her social standing."

"Oui, but I think she has her eye on you, you lucky devil! Ah, to be young again."

"Give her another chance, Gaston. What the hell, you're still sort of distinguished, right?"

Gaston rose with a snort and said, "That is what I mean. Youth is so wasted on the young. But very well. If all else fails, I can pull a gun on her, non?"

Gaston wandered back to camp. Captain Gringo sat there smoking and listening for a long time. The swamp was silent, save for the occasional grunt of a bull 'gator in the distance. With luck it was mating with old Diego. The asshole was sure to be picked up on his own if he made it back to dry land. Could he lead anyone back to them? Not far. And if there were any soldados close, they were already in trouble.

Old Tio Julio came out to join him an hour or so later. Julio asked if his nephew had returned. Captain Gringo said, "No, and I don't think he will. He's been gone quite a while. Any ideas on which way he might have headed, Julio?"

"He said something about searching for mangrove fruit, over to the east, my captain."

"Oh, shit. I might have known. Okay, if he made the coastal salt marshes he got lost coming back. They can't be that far. Try it another way. Could he work back to that fishing village along the dry ground between us and the coast mangroves?"

"Perhaps. But why would he wish for to do that? Those soldados were going to shoot him at sunrise too!"

"I noticed. Diego might not have. No offense, viejo, but your nephew isn't too bright."

"Alas, I know. I told my late sister I would look after the boy. But what can one do with a spoiled mocoso who's already overgrown you when you get him?"

"Nada. Go catch some sleep, Julio. It's very late and we have a long way to wade, come sunrise."

The old man went back to flop on his thatch. Another million years went by and Captain Gringo began to miss him. He knew the other pickets were as bored, if they were still awake. He got up, circled, and told each of the men he stumbled over to return to camp and kick someone awake to take their places. He sat on the same log a spell, tried again, and found that his casual guard mount had worked. Better yet, the new men were bright-eyed and interested in staring out at nothing much. A lot they knew. The biggest problem in keeping a night watch was that ninety-nine times out of a hundred, nothing happened. After a guy had pulled guard a few times he stopped expecting anything to happen. And that was when Washington usually crossed the Delaware.

He was having trouble with his own eyelids when Gaston came back to say, "Eh bien. It is, almost dawn and I am up again for the day. Bless you, my child. I never could have done it without you."

"Oh? How was she?

"Très fantastique. I think she was trying to prove some obscure point. I asked why she was so passionate. But she could not talk with her mouth filled. How did you know she put out? I refrained from paying her the same oral compliments until I had a chance to ask you."

Captain Gringo laughed and got to his feet, stamping one foot to wake it up as he said, "I didn't get any, if we're talking about the redhead. I've never enjoyed cat fights. Wake me up at first light, Gaston. I want to move us out of this neck of the woods poco tiempo in case that dumb Diego has been picked up and knows how to draw maps."

"Mon Dieu, the idiot doesn't have to. He knows we are making for that British base at Greytown, non?"

"Yeah; if he doesn't come back with a mouth full of mangrove fruit, we'd better make for someplace else."

"Is there someplace else, Dick?"

"Beats me. But either way we can't stay here. We have to find some food, and more supplies wouldn't hurt either."

He started to leave. Gaston stopped him and lowered his voice to say, "Listen, I've been thinking. If the two of us forged on, right now . . ."

"Damm it, everyone around here keeps *thinking*!" Captain Gringo cut in, adding, "The moon is setting. It's going to get darker before it gets lighter, and there's at least one big bull 'gator out there somewhere. Besides, I thought you liked redheads."

"Oh, I do, now. But not enough to die for one. We're never going to get anywhere with this ragtag band of amateurs, Dick!"

"That's all right. We don't have anyplace to go."

Captain Gringo returned to his lean-to and Consuela. It was getting cold now, but the pretty little Mestiza was awake and hot. As he lay down beside her on the thatch in the dark, Consuela said, "Hold me close and keep me warm, toro mio. Did you know that stuck-up redhead across the way was just being very naughty with your friend Gaston?"

"You're kidding. How do you know? Did you strike a match?"

She giggled and whispered, "I didn't have to. She was giving everyone in earshot a blow-by-blow description, and he is noisy, too! Take off your pants, querido. Now it's my turn to show off, no?"

He started feeling her up as she fumbled at his belt, but said, "No. We have to be discreet. Not for Rubia. For the others. We may not have enough willing women to go around, and next to watching two women fight, there's nothing more tedious for a commanding officer than breaking up fights among his troops."

She got his pants off. She was already nude, of course, as she said, "I think most of the others have paired off. All but a few of the uglier men, anyway. That Hachismo was pestering me earlier. But I told him I was your adelita, so . . .''

"Oh boy. He's one of the tough ones, too! Okay, doll box, I'll get on top this time, but let's keep it to ourselves, eh? It's cruelty to animals to remind them someone's getting something they can't have.''

She tried. Probably nobody but Rubia across the way heard when Consuela moaned she was coming.

He did, too, but only once this time. He had a lot on his mind and needed rest more than he needed anything else. He wouldn't have bothered at all if Consuela hadn't been awake and Rubia hadn't gotten him hard. He started to wonder if the unseen redhead was as curious about what they might have missed as he was. Even after laying Consuela, he was still curious. But what the hell, Gaston was a pal, and piggy guys wound up getting shot a lot.

He'd dozed off a while with Consuela in his arms and her skirt pulled up over them when Gaston woke them, whispering, "Rise and shine, my children. One can see one's hand before one's face again, and it may be more serious than that!''

Captain Gringo asked what he meant as he sat up to pull on his pants and gunbelt. Gaston said, "I thought I heard something out in the swamp to the east just now.''

The younger soldier of fortune snapped wide awake as Gaston added, "I might have heard distant shouting. I know I heard splashing, as if someone had fallen in the water. One tends to trip over roots in this light, non?''

Consuela was still half-asleep. Captain Gringo shook her and told her to get dressed as he reached across her for the machine gun. He trailed the ammo belt across her naked belly as he rose to his feet with it and told Gaston to wake the others quietly and get everybody flat, with the women in the center of the hammock and the men facing the swamp all around with their rifles, prone. He added, "You move around and keep an eye on our flanks and rear. I'll set up facing the mystery splashes.''

Not waiting to discuss it further, Captain Gringo toted the Maxim to the east side of the hammock, found another fallen log, and braced it across it to face the east. Gaston had been right about the light. He could see maybe fifty feet out across the dark water between the cypress trees. By the time he'd smoked half a cigar he could see farther. The sun was coming up and some birds were raising hell about it above his head. He muttered, ''Shut up, birds! This could be serious!''

The birds just got louder. But now he could hear an occasional distant shout. Someone was coming, sure as hell. It sounded like a long skirmish line, keeping contact by calling back and forth as they moved abreast in the knee-deep water. He armed the Maxim, chewing the butt of his smoke after snuffing the tip out on the log. Trained troops wouldn't be advancing so sloppily. On the other hand, how many troops down here had ever been to the Point?

Gaston joined him, flopping beside him to hold the ammo belt as he said, ''Eh bien, everyone is in position, and anyone can tell those noisy children are moving in from the east, non?''

''Yeah, and whoever they are, they know the way. They're coming right at us. What do you think. Soldados or ladrónes?''

Gaston shrugged and asked, ''There is a difference? Ah, I just spotted a flash of white cotton. Over to your right, Dick.''

''Yeah, I saw it too. That fucking big tree is in the way now. I hope you told everyone to hold his fire?''

''Oui. They are not to shoot anyone before they see the whites of their eyes and all that. Perhaps I should have said the whites of their peon pants. The light is trés tricky this early.''

As if to prove Gaston a liar, a distant patch of white started waving at them and a faraway voice called out, ''Hola!, that island! Do not shoot, señores! We wish for a parley! Is it agreeable?"

Captain Gringo called back, "Advance and be recognized. Small parley party with hands polite!"

Three figures detached themselves from the trees they'd been taking cover behind and moved closer, one waving the white flag wildly as he called in a familiar voice, "It is all right, Captain Gringo! These hombres wish for to join us!"

"Let's hear the story, Diego!"

"They are, like us, fugitives from those crazy soldados. I met them as I searched for food. I had to have something to eat."

"We'll talk about that later. What have you got there?"

One of the men with Diego moved closer to call out, "We are guerrillas like yourselves, señores. We wish for to be your compañeros! Is it true you have guns and . . . women?"

"We have enough for ourselves. Not enough to share. How many in your party and, more important, what have you got to put in the pot?"

The outlaw spokesman laughed and replied, "We have guns and ammo. We have food. We have no women and no dinero. But our requirements are modest. This señorito says you got a dozen women. Maybe we take half off your hands, eh?"

"It won't work. There are ten men in my band. Or nine, if Diego is with you. How about it, Diego? You want to come home to Tio Julio?"

Diego didn't answer. Gaston muttered, "I think they're covering the boy," and Captain Gringo replied, "Tell me something I didn't know. Any suggestions?"

Captain Gringo counted to ten under his breath to give the impression he was discussing the idea with someone as dumb as they thought he was. Then he called back, "All right, as long as I have your word, and remember, no tricks!"

The spokesman in sight turned to wave his companions

closer, and as they broke cover Gaston whistled and said, "Merde alors! There must be fifty of them!"

"I noticed. When I open up, see if you can drop Diego without killing him. I think we may owe him."

"Owe him what, a kick in the balls? He led those ladrónes right to us!"

"Yeah. Most guys would have, in his spot. If he'd warned them about this machine gun they wouldn't be coming in like that. That's a skirmish line meant to rush a handful of riflemen, period."

"Ah, oui, a pistol ball in the thigh should heal quickly."

The spokesman figured to be the leader as well, from the way he was acting now. He'd lagged behind Diego and the parley flag as he urged his followers on, calling out, "Go ashore and dry your feet, muchachos. The señores know we are friendly, eh?"

Captain Gringo saw he wasn't coming any closer before he ordered the charge. So he muttered, "Up yours, you friendly son of a bitch!" and opened fire.

The results of his first traverse surprised the shit out of the ladrónes, although Captain Gringo was mildly disappointed with the results and had to traverse back to churn skirmish line and swamp water into pink froth. The nicest thing to be said about cutting a guy off at the knees in knee-deep water was that once you dropped him good, he tended to stay down. A wounded man screaming and rolling around could drown in surprisingly shallow water. But some of the pricks managed to get off a few rounds of small-arms fire before he could drop them. A bullet spanged off the log between him and Gaston as Gaston, too, fired his pistol into the confusion.

The Maxim choked on the end of the empty ammo belt. Captain Gringo swore and drew his thumb-buster. But when he aimed it out across the water, there was no target. It made little sense to fire at a shirt bobbing gently in the roiled swamp water. He said, "I think a couple could have made it out the back door. See Diego out there anywhere?"

"Oui; he did not make it anywhere. That's him, face down by the floating white flag."

"Damn it, Gaston . . ."

"Damn me no damns, you noisy child. I didn't do it. You didn't do it. Regard the blossom of crimson between his soggy shoulder blades, hein?"

"Oh, right. I thought they were covering him. Must have thought he'd betrayed them. They thought right. The kid was okay after all."

The silence had attracted some of the other men. Captain Gringo started to chew them out for deserting their positions. Then he spotted old Julio and said soberly, "They were ladrónes. They captured Diego and forced him to lead them to us. But your nephew died a hero, Tio Julio. He didn't tell them about this machine gun."

The old man made the sign of the cross as he sighed and said, "The boy was always delicate. I thank God he died like an hombre. Which one is he?"

Captain Gringo pointed and said, "Over there. Shot in the back. We'll bury him with full honors here. The 'gators can have the others. But let's get to work and salvage them for pistols, ammo, and any other goodies they have on 'em. I need some .30-30 rounds. A lot of .30-30 rounds, if I ever want to use this machine gun again. Oh, yeah, see if any of them were packing gun oil, and we can use canteens, too."

One of the girls they'd told to take cover in the middle of the hammock came to join them with a sad little face. She said, "Captain Gringo, you had better come with me. Your adelita, Consuela, needs you."

"Tell her later. I'm sort of tied up right now, ah . . . ?"

"I am called Lolita. I do not think Consuela can wait until later. She has been shot. We think she is dying!"

He gasped, said, "Right!" and followed Lolita to where Consuela lay with her head in Rubia's lap. Rubia was crying. She looked up bleakly and said, "I told her to stay down. When she heard the shooting she sprang up to run to your assistance, the poor little fool!"

Captain Gringo dropped to his knees in the sand beside the wounded adelita and took her hand in his. Consuela opened her eyes, smiled wanly up at him, and asked, "Deek, do you think I am pretty?"

"Honey, you're the prettiest little thing there ever was," he replied, moving the bottom of her blouse for a better look at the bullet hole in her bare midriff. From her pallor, most of the bleeding was internal. She said, "Tell me once more I am pretty, toro mio." So he did. She said, "I am so happy," just as she stopped breathing, still staring up adoringly at him.

He gently closed her eyes, swore softly under his breath, and told Rubia, "You can lower her head to the sand now, Rubia. We'll bury her and Diego together."

"I think the little fool really loved you," said Rubia, in a voice tinged with soft wonder. Captain Gringo got up, walked over to a tree, and punched it until his knuckles bled.

It didn't help a bit.

It was almost noon by the time they floundered up onto the dry strip between the inland fresh-water swamps and the saline mangrove swamps stretching eastward to hide the seaward horizon. Dry was a relative term along any part of the Mosquito Coast. The north-south cuesta was a line of stabilized dunes, covered with palmetto, sea grape, wild plum, and, if you were dumb, poisonous machineel. The sun could get at the coral sand between the scrubby dry-root trees. So one couldn't see much sand for the shin-high ground cover of creepers and dune grass. A lot of the creeping crud was armed with thorns, and a snake or scorpion could be almost anywhere, but the peones had tough feet, and at least they were dry for a change as they forged south.

The soggier battlefield behind had yielded several hundred rounds of ammo, tobacco money for everyone in Captain Gringo's band, a dozen canteens, and a nice double-action .38 complete with shoulder rig.

Captain Gringo had put it on and given the thumb-buster to Hachismo, who said he knew how to use a six-gun.

At one or two, judging by the sun since they had no timepieces, they came to a tidal creek cutting them off from the high ground to the south. The tide was at ebb. So Captain Gringo led his people to the other side through waist-deep water before he called a siesta break.

On the way across, Perrito caught a salt-water croc' by the tail and hauled it, thrashing, up on the bank for Hachismo to try the six-gun on. The six-gun worked swell. So they cut the croc' up and ate it. It was only fair, since as Hachismo pointed out, the bastard would have eaten one of them if he hadn't spotted it in time. The firm white meat tasted better than anything any of them had eaten for forty-odd hours, although Captain Gringo at least waited until he'd broiled his share of the tail over the siesta fire. Some of the others weren't so picky. None of the wild plums they'd passed had been in fruit.

Gaston hunkered down beside Captain Gringo as the tall American set up a hasty machine-gun nest covering the tidal creek they'd just crossed. Gaston belched and said, "Eh bien, that was hardly tenderloin, but I begin to feel human again. Do you still think we are being followed, my nervous youth?"

Captain Gringo said, "No. But why take chances? Do you have any smokes left? I've used up all mine."

Gaston took a soggy claro from his shirt and said, "Here, this is the last one. You can have it."

"Oh, hell, it's covered with blood, Gaston."

"Oui, that's why I hadn't smoked it yet. I don't think the swamp water did it much good either."

Captain Gringo threw it away, saying, "It had to be crawling with all kinds of jungle crud. We'll hole up here during the heat of the afternoon. You want to send some foragers over into the mangroves? Mangrove fruit ain't much, but we can't hope to shoot a croc' every time we stop for a break."

Gaston said, "I don't have to detail anyone to forage. The boys are already turning over the thatch all about for lizards, yucca roots, and other distressing staples of the local diet. Don't worry. Now that we're on dry ground, the food situation should improve. Have you ever tried scorpion in a vinegar sauce, Dick?"

"Glugh. I tasted one of those big sugared cockroaches the Mexicans find so tasty, once. Remind me never to do that again."

"True. Palm grubs are less complicated to bone. Do you have any idea where we might be on the map, Dick?"

"No. Hopefully nobody else does either. If we keep pushing south we ought to hit a crossroad leading to Greytown."

"And if we do not?"

"We could hardly miss the Rio San Juan."

"Not true, my intrepid explorer. The river between Nicaragua and Costa Rica meets the sea in a blasé manner. The estuary is lined with considerable stretches of salt marsh. This jolly ridgeway must end long before we reach the San Juan, and, aside from salt-water crocodilians, have you forgotten the fresh-to-brackish-water sharks we met that time on Lake Nicaragua?"

"Who could forget? They damn near ate us when we had to swim for it that time. Yeah, you're right. We'd better try for Greytown. At least our Hispanic pals will be okay there, and we can always stick poker chips in our eyes and hope to pass for English beachcombers long enough to hop a boat out.''

"With what for money, my eternal optimist? If we robbed everyone in our gang we wouldn't have enough to bribe a thirsty deckhand!''

Captain Gringo snorted in disgust and said, "Hey, don't cross your bridges until you come to them. We still have to get to Greytown before we have to worry about picky details. If we overshoot, I don't know what the fuck we're supposed to do!''

Gaston brightened and said, "Speaking of fucking, I wonder if Rubia would like to take a stroll down the coast with me. Have you thought about a replacement for Consuela yet?''

"No. Go get laid and let *me* worry about my sex life, you horny old bastard.''

Gaston laughed and scampered off to take him up on the suggestion. It was getting hot, but no doubt they'd find a shady spot. Captain Gringo left the Maxim to bake dry in the sun as he moved under a palmetto and leaned his back against the rough trunk in the modest shade. It was already getting dull as hell, and he knew they shouldn't move until at least three or four.

He sat a time alone, staring north across the tidal creek. Then the girl called Lolita joined him and asked, "Is it permitted for me to sit down, Señor Deek?''

He nodded, and she hiked her skirt to drop to her knees in the dry grass beside him. She was neither prettier nor uglier than the late Consuela, and not nearly as attractive as the redheaded Rubia, damn Gaston's hide. Lolita looked like a vague relative of the Mestiza they'd buried back on the hammock with Diego. She was a little plumper and not quite as brown. Her big almond eyes were nice. They looked worried as she said, "I wish for to speak with you in private, señor. That ladrón, Hachismo, has been talking about you behind your back."

He nodded wearily and said, "So now you're talking behind his back and that makes you even, Lolita."

"Do not you wish for to know what Hachismo has been saying to the other hombres?"

"I already know. One of the things that makes running a guerrilla band so tiresome is that everybody wants to be a chief and nobody wants to be an Indian."

"Oh, you knew he was suggesting he knew the country and the ways of our people better than you, Señor Deek?"

"Sure. He's right, too. Just call me Dick, doll. Am I guessing right again when I suppose you haven't lined up a soldado yet?"

She giggled and said, "It is true. You *do* read minds! As a matter of fact, Hachismo suggested I should be his adelita. I do not wish for to be his adelita. He is very ugly."

"That's funny, another muchacha was telling me the same thing about the poor slob. Okay, as long as we're going to gossip. I make it nine men and eleven women in our party now. That leaves at least two of you ladies out, right?"

"Sí, and I am prettier than Gordita. Hachismo could have Gordita. But I do not think he wants her."

He thought, and said, "Yeah, Gordita's the fat girl with the skin problem, right?"

"Sí. She does not really have the pox, it just looks like she has. I think, before we were all arrested, Gordita ate too much chocolate."

"Well, we've got her on a healthy diet now. Is everyone but Hachismo and me fixed up?"

"More or less. Those couples who have not exchanged promises are at least flirting only with one another, now. Is it true you are a most brutal lover, Deek?"

"Who told you that, Rubia?"

"Sí, she told us you almost raped her in the Italian manner."

"I thought it was Greek. I thought she'd stop making trouble once I found a soldado for her. Don't worry about it. I'm not going to rape any of you in any manner."

"Oh, I am so relieved. Is it permitted for me to march with you when we move on? I fear I told Hachismo a little fib. Only to make him stop bothering me. I meant no disrespect."

He closed his eyes, leaned his head back against the trunk, and muttered, "Oh boy! Hachismo's one of my few decent fighters, too! What did you tell him, that you were my adelita?"

"Sort of. I said we were still discussing the matter, since Consuela is barely cold in her grave back there."

He shook his head warily and said, "Don't ever do that to a man with the hots for you, Lolita. A man can drop it if he knows for sure he's out of the picture. You left Hachismo's foot in the door by leaving our relationship up in the air."

"I'm sorry. What can I do to make amends?"

"I'm thinking. You're sure he's not your type? I may not stick around as long as a native Nicaraguan, you know. Old Hachismo may not be pretty, but he's a born survivor and may wind up buying you lots of play-pretties when things settle down and he's back in the stick-'em-up business again."

She shook her head stubbornly and insisted she'd rather die than give herself to such a horrid person. That was probably a slight exaggeration. Prettier girls than she gave themselves regularly to Apache when the old fate-worse-than-death shit was put to the real test. But it looked like Hachismo would do better with someone else at the moment. He'd be more apt to settle even for the fat girl if he knew for sure Lolita was a lost cause. So Captain Gringo told Lolita, "All right. We may as well make it official. Nobody's in sight. Take off your clothes."

Lolita gasped and said, "Por favor! I am not a woman to be treated as a puta!"

"So what kind of woman are you, a common prick-tease? I never asked you to be my adelita, damn it. You volunteered. Don't you know the duties of an adelita?"

"Sí, an adelita carries her soldado's pack and cooks his food for him. If he is wounded she takes care of him. If he is killed, she avenges him. If they march well together, they may even get married someday when the war is over. It is all very romantico, no?"

"Oh, hell. You've been listening to revolutionary songs and not paying attention to the lyrics, I see. All bullshit aside, kid, are you still a damn virgin?"

Lolita started to cry, staring down at her own hands as she twisted the hem of her thin skirt in her lap. He growled, "Never mind. Stupid question. Cut the blubbering, Lolita. I'm sorry if I shocked you. I didn't know you were a family girl."

"I am sorry. Forgive me. I am new at guerrilla warfare, Deek. Does this mean I cannot be your adelita?"

He started to tell her she was asking stupid questions now. Then he reconsidered. A young cherry had to be protected, and it wasn't as if he meant to spend the rest of his life with this gang. With luck, he and Gaston would be rid of them in a few days at the most. Meanwhile, his life was complicated enough. His voice was gentler as he said, "Stop sniffling. We can say you're my adelita. That ought to cheer Gordita up when nature takes its disgusting course. God, what an ugly couple she and Hachismo make."

Lolita giggled and said, "I find it obscene, and I am not sure I know just what they have to do to each other at night. I am so glad I may tell everyone I am your adelita now, Deek."

"I wish you wouldn't. Just march with me as we move out and let word get around. We're going to have to fake things a little, Lolita. You can't tell the other women we're, ah, still platonic friends.''

She blanched and asked, ''Do you wish them to think I am immoral?''

''Hey, back up and stop changing the rules, damn it! If you want them to think you're my woman, you'll have to let 'em think what they want. I won't take advantage of you, but you mustn't make them think I'm a sissy, either. Is any of this sinking in, Lolita?''

''I think so. You wish everyone to think we are being vile at night. But I do not know how to act vile, Deek.''

''Not to worry. Who looks when the lights are out? Just hang around and make yourself useful with the camp chores and so forth. You're not big enough to pack my machine gun and I hardly have anything else for you to carry. I'm easy as hell on adelitas.''

Nobody commented, at first, when they moved out late that afternoon. But he could see the message had been noted as Lolita trudged at his side mile after mile, with old Julio and a guy called Paco spelling each other on the Maxim behind them. Hachismo, bringing up the rear, didn't see fit to notice. Some of the other women shot Lolita congratulatory glances, and the redhead, Rubia, looked bewildered as well as mad as hell about something.

They made good time. Even better, Gaston, out on point, flushed a key deer at sundown and downed it with a snap shot from his army rifle. That was as good an excuse as any to stop.

As a couple of peones cut up the venison and the women built fires, Captain Gringo called the men together and announced, ''We'll eat and rest awhile. Then we'll push on until the moon goes down and make a more permanent night camp. Any questions?"

Hachismo said, with a scowl, "Sí, I have *many* questions, Yanqui. For why do we have to push on at all? Do you have any idea where you are leading us?"

Captain Gringo said, "Greytown. The English colony's not having a civil war this season. I'm willing to listen if anyone has a better suggestion."

Hachismo's voice dripped honey and venom as he replied, "Oh, the great one is willing to listen to his inferiors?"

Captain Gringo raised an eyebrow and silently signaled Gaston to keep out of it as the little Frenchman started to circle around behind Hachismo, scratching the back of his neck with a puzzled smile. Captain Gringo's smile was less innocent as he said, "I listen to anyone who has anything sensible to say, Hachismo. Cut the sarcasm and get to the point, if you have one. Don't you like the idea of a run for Greytown?"

Hachismo shrugged and said, "I know nothing about the English there. I do not wish for to know anything about the English there. I spit in the milk of their mothers. Sí, I spit in the milk of *all* Anglo's mothers!"

"You must spit a lot, Hachismo. How do you manage that with your mouth hanging open like that? Hasn't anyone ever told you the open mouth catches flies?"

The other men, being Hispanic, knew a not-too-veiled death threat when they heard one. Hachismo found himself facing Captain Gringo solo as the others moved warily out of the line of fire.

Captain Gringo didn't want it to end seriously. He said, "I don't know why you're trying to provoke me, amigo. Before this gets silly, why don't you just say right out what's bothering you?"

A man in the crowd murmured, "That is fair, Hachismo. Tell the man what you told us before."

Hachismo scuffed at the sand with his foot and growled, "I do not know whether to start in a numerical or alphabetical manner. This gringo took the machine-gun for himself. He took that nice .38 for himself. He even takes all the pussy for himself!"

"Careful, muchacho, you are not referring to my adelita, I hope."

"Fuck your adelita! Fuck your mother, too, you gringo bastard!"

Having gone that far, Hachismo knew, of course, it was time to go for his gun. But Captain Gringo had grown accustomed to the folk ways of Latin America. So he was going for his own gun at the same time. He beat the hatchet-faced ladrón to the draw, just, and what the hell, as long as he was shooting him, he might as well do it right.

Hachismo went over backward with the old thumb-buster in his hand, a wistful expression on his ugly dead face, and a row of four red bullet holes gushing from his cotton shirt. He'd barely hit the ground when Gaston had his own gun out and was saying pleasantly, "Everybody freeze!"

Captain Gringo chided, "Now, now, we're all friends here, Gaston."

There was a chorus of agreement, and one man volunteered, "The pobrecito must have gone loco en la cabeza! Everyone knows it is suicide to draw a single-action from a side holster against a double-action in a shoulder holster."

Perrito, the other obvious bandito with them, stepped silently over to the corpse, squatted, and took the buscadero rig and thumb-buster for himself as he asked, "Do you wish us to bury him, my captain? Or can we just leave him for the birds?"

Captain Gringo finished reloading and put his .38 away as he said, "Bury him. He was a comrade in arms, up until he went crazy from the heat."

The women, of course, had come over to see what was

going on by now. Little Lolita ran to Captain Gringo and asked, "Are you wounded, soldado mio?"

He said, "No. Sorry. How's supper coming along?"

Gordita, the fat girl, stared pensively down at the body of Hachismo and said, "The venison is well browned on the outside. But we shall all get sick if we eat too much. Venison should hang at least overnight before one eats it. For why did someone kill Hachismo?"

"He went crazy with love, I think. The rest of you heard what Gordita said, and she's right. Eat just enough of that green meat to settle your innards. We'll pack some along after smoking it. This is no time to come down with the trots. We'll be pushing on in about an hour."

The moon fizzled out after midnight. Captain Gringo ordered no fires as they bedded down as best they could in scattered nests of dry grass. The stars looked close enough to reach up and grab by the handful, so there was no point in building palmetto shelters. It was even colder on the moderately high ground with the trades blowing in from the sea. The wind helped with the bugs, albeit not enough for total comfort. With salt marshes to the east and fresh-water swamps to the west, they got the mosquitoes doublebarreled, depending on the eddies near ground level. It was a toss-up whether salt- or fresh-water mosquitoes were worse. The big salt-marsh species bit deeper and perhaps less often. The fresh-water jobs made up for their smaller size by numerical mass, and drove everyone nuts by humming like hell whether they meant to bite or not. Most of them did.

Captain Gringo made a public display of bedding down with Lolita in a clump of gumbo limbo. As soon as things settled down, he whispered to her that it was time to move. She got up. No problem since they were fully dressed and

had no bedclothes, but as he held her hand to lead her
through the darkness, she asked where they were going, and
why.

He found a clean patch of sand by starlight and feel, and
started throwing together a pillow of dry grass as he explained,
"Never sleep where a dead man's friends might be expecting
you to sleep, doll."

She dropped beside him and sobbed, "Oh, my God, are
we in danger?"

"You just noticed? Don't get upset. I'm just taking stand-
ard precautions. I don't know if anyone else wants to start up
with me or not. It hurts less when you find out some easier
way than taking a shot or a stab in the dark. Stretch out and
get some sleep, muchacha. We have a long day ahead of us.
With luck, we're almost there. I keep expecting to hit a
crossroad leading to Greytown. It's gotta be *somewhere*
around here. We're running out of country. Boy, I sure hope
we haven't overshot Greytown!"

She lay full length in the sand with her head and shoulders
on the thatch as she asked, "Is it possible to miss such a big
colony, Deek?"

He said, "It's easy. Greytown's a British navy base and
trading post. I'm not even sure they *have* a road leading
inland. Your various Nicaraguan governments keep asking
Queen Victoria to vacate the premises. I sure hope nobody's been listening since the last time I read the *London
Times*."

She obviously didn't know what he was talking about. She
stared up at him in the dim light and asked, "Why are you
still sitting up? Do not you wish for to sleep, too?"

He said, "I will, before morning. Anyone plotting anything should spring the trap pretty soon, if they're ever going
to."

"Trap, soldado mio?"

"Oh, I keep forgetting you're new at this. Yeah, I bent

some of that springy gumbo limbo to snap up loud if anyone should pussy-foot into that clump we said nighty-night from before.''

"Heavens, you are so clever, Deek. For how did you get to be such a sneaky person?''

He shrugged and said, "Okay, you want a bedtime story? Once upon a time there was a nice dumb U.S. Cavalry officer named Dick Walker. He came out west from the Point thinking the world was run on the level. Even after he'd chased Apache for a while he was still pretty dumb. He'd learned all sorts of sneaky Indian tricks by then, but he still thought you could trust fellow officers. He found out the hard way he couldn't. One day they needed a scapegoat for the mistakes of some stupid brass. Guess who got to take the blame at a rigged court-martial?''

"I do not know, Deek. Forgive me. I do not know what you are talking about.''

"That's okay, they didn't know what they were talking about either. But they still found me guilty and sentenced me to hang.''

"Someone tried to hang you, Deek? That sounds very cruel!''

"I thought so too. So I didn't hang around for my hanging. I had to kill one of the pricks who'd helped to frame me as I took my leave of the old Tenth Cav. I jumped the border, and, what do you know, some Mexicans wanted to kill me too. They had a noisier execution in mind, but no matter. Gaston and I escaped together. I think we upset the Mexican federales as we shot our way out of the country. They were the ones who first called me Captain Gringo. Actually I was only an ordinance officer with the rank of first lieutenant when I was forced to become a renegade, or soldier of fortune, depending on who's out to collect the reward or hire me to shoot somebody else. You still awake? Okay, have you heard the one about the three bears?''

Something snapped, not far away. He hissed, "Don't make a sound!" and rolled to his feet, pistol in hand, to move in on whoever had sprung his gumbo-limbo trap.

It was Rubia. He almost shot the silly redhead in the dim light before he saw it was her coming out of the gumbo limbo. She wasn't packing any weapons. In fact, she was naked as a jaybird. He holstered his .38 and said, "Evening, red. I assume Gaston's asleep?"

She said, "Oh, it's you. You startled me!"

"I hope so. Why were you pussy-footing around in there, red? I can see murder couldn't have been your motive."

The redhead laughed brazenly and said, "I was hoping Lolita would be sleeping too. You can't seriously mean to abuse that poor child with that big thing of yours, Deek! I can't allow it. It's inhuman."

"Oh, I don't know. She hasn't screamed loud enough to wake anyone else up, I see. What's your problem, insomnia or nymphomania?"

"Let us say it may be a little of both. Gaston is all right. Surprisingly virile for a man his age, in fact. But I am a woman of passion, Deek. I need lots of sex, and, to tell the truth, I suffer from a normal woman's curiosity."

"Normal my ass! You must be curious as a barrel of cats if you're creeping around bare ass at this hour. What's to be curious about? You've already fondled my dong."

She chuckled and reached out for him again as she husked, "Sí, and I think I may have made a terrible mistake. If I let you, well, abuse me as you wish, do you promise to finish in me the old-fashioned way?"

It was tempting. It wasn't as if he and Gaston hadn't passed around the goodies now and again. But Gaston could be old-fashioned too. He'd go for a swap. But poor little Lolita might not be as sophisticated as Rubia.

He smiled down at the naked redhead and said, "Not

tonight, Josephine. I've got someone to sleep with, and you ain't it.''

"Have you already had all you want of that child?"

He nodded. It was true enough, when you thought about it.

Rubia moved closer, plastered her lush naked flesh against him, and reached down to feel him up as she purred, "Liar! You're stiff as a poker right now!"

He laughed and said, "Son of a bitch if I'm not. Well, it's been nice talking to you, red. But I'd better go back and put this old horny rascal where he belongs. Honeymoon night and all that stuff, you know. I'll see you around the campus, doll box."

"Listen, I'll take it in the derriere for you, darling!"

"Sorry. Already have one of those things waiting for me, and she may be starting to worry about me."

"Deek, I'm *curious*! I know I behaved like a schoolgirl the other night, but I've been wondering ever since what it would feel like in me that way, so . . ."

"Ask Gaston to show you. He served a hitch in North Africa."

She would have asked again, but he'd turned and vanished into the darkness, muttering, "Why me, God? What did I do to deserve a crazy redhead begging to be cornholed and a dumb little virgin who doesn't want it at all? Haven't you any sense of moderation, damm it?"

When he rejoined Lolita, she naturally asked who'd been trying to murder him. He didn't want her to lose sleep over needless worry, so he said, "False alarm. One of the other girls tripped my noise trap by accident."

"Oh? What was another woman doing in our bed, Deek?"

"It wasn't our bed. It was an empty clump of gumbo limbo. Lie back down and go to sleep."

She didn't. She reclined on one elbow, pouting, as she said, "I am not *that* innocent! If another woman was creeping into bed with you, or thought she was, she was trying for to steal my soldado! Who was it, Gordita? I'll scratch that fat cow's eyes out if she tries to steal my soldado!''

He laughed and said, "It wasn't Gordita and that's all you're going to get out of me. I don't want you fighting with the other girls over me. This whole thing's already too silly to believe!''

"I know she was silly. You are *my* soldado, God strike her selfish you-know-what! What was the matter with her? Doesn't she have anyone for to be vile with?''

He chuckled and said, "She's been vile as hell, most likely. I guess some women can't get enough from one poor brute. Forget it, Lolita. It's over and no damage done.''

She did no such thing. She moved closer and asked, "Are you sure you were not vile with her, just now? How did you satisfy her if you were not vile?''

"I don't imagine I did satisfy her. Do we have to continue this dumb conversation, Lolita? In the first place, what you keep harping on isn't all that vile. In the second place, it's unsettling to keep harping on it at all. A man has feelings, you know.''

She pouted and said, "I know. My mother told me all you men wanted to be vile with women every chance you got.''

"I'm sure your mother led a very happy life. Shut up and go to sleep.''

"Hah! Now I know you were vile with that other woman! My mother said men never speak rudely to a woman unless they do not feel like treating her with savagery!''

"Oh boy! I wish your mother were here right now. I'd kick her in the ass for openers! Look, sweet and stupid, I don't care if you believe me or not. A guy can't cheat on a dame he's not involved with, so what possible difference could it make to you if I fooled around with, hell, old fat Gordita or Queen Victoria in the flesh?''

She started to cry. He took her in his arms and soothed,

"Okay, okay, I was kidding. I haven't been vile with anybody, okay?"

She snuggled against his chest and sniffed, "I wish I could believe you, but how can a woman be sure her *soldado* has not been vile with another *adelita*?"

He started to tell her she couldn't. Then he unbuttoned his fly, hauled out his raging erection, and moved her hand down to it, asking with a grin, "There. Feel that and tell me I've just fired it in recent action!"

She gasped, but held on as she said, "Oh, this can't be a proper way to behave, Deek! Should I be touching you like this?"

"Well, no, as a matter of fact it would feel better if you sort of moved your hand back and forth, like this."

She started shyly to jerk him off as she murmured, "Oh, it feels nothing like my mother said it would. It doesn't feel vile at all. Just a little naughty, I think."

He held her closer and ran his own hand under her skirt as he kissed her. She started jerking him harder as she responded to his kiss with the childlike innocence of her inexperience combining with dawning instincts that really don't require many lessons. So as he got his hand in position to stroke her moist slit, she only asked, "Are you trying to be vile?" and didn't struggle as he assured her, "Not at all. I'm just trying to find out if you feel vile or just naughty down there."

She said, "Oh. Well, what do you think? Do I feel disgusting to you between my thighs, Deek?"

"I'm not sure yet. How does it feel to you?"

She frowned thoughtfully and said, "Not nearly as bad as my mother said it would. Ah, could you move a little faster, *soldado mio*? Something very interesting seems to be happening and I'm not sure if I like it or not but I think I do, I know I do, and, oh, my God, what is happeninggggggg!"

She started to struggle mindlessly, but he held her, firmly albeit gently, until he'd massaged her to climax and then drove two fingers in to let her come back to her senses contracting nicely on them. By now she'd stopped stroking him. But when next they kissed, she tongued him instinctively as he lowered her gently to the sand and took her up on the unspoken invitation, whether she'd meant it as one or not, by rolling between her thighs, pulling her skirt out of the way, and doing what came naturally. He came so hard he damn near blew his socks off.

As they lay there together, Lolita opened her eyes dreamily and asked, "Is this what they call fucking, Deek?"

So, since she didn't seem to find it all that vile, he started moving in her again as he assured her gently, "That's a crude way of putting it, but yeah, that's what we seem to be doing all right."

She said, "Oh, dear, my mother told me never to do this with anyone unless we were married, and only then when he forced me to."

"Do you feel forced, Lolita?"

"Sí, a little. But it is not as vile as my mother said it would be. As a matter of fact, I am beginning to wonder what my poor mother was talking about. I do not mind this at all. I think, in fact, oh, yes, yes, do it faster, querido mio! That funny feeling is coming over me again and it feels even better *this* way!"

So he made her come, stripped her to the buff, and did it three more times before he began to feel like a shit. When he told her he was sorry for taking her cherry, Lolita said, "I do not feel like I lost anything, Deek. I seem to have *found* something, and it feels so good in there. I think maybe my mother did not do it right. Or maybe my papa did not do it as you do. Now that I am your true adelita, you will teach me *all* the ways to be vile, no? I like it, no matter what my mother says."

He stopped to get his breath back, dying for a smoke, and began by counting the days of the month with her until he saw they didn't have to worry about that. She said, "So *that* is how the older girls managed that part? Oh, I have so much to learn, and you are such a good teacher. Tell me, Deek, what is this French business the older women giggle so about?"

He laughed and said, "We'll save linguistics for another lesson. Right now, no bull, we'd really better try and get some sleep. We seem to have screwed half the night away."

She said, "I know, and it makes me feel so happy."

The next two days on the trail were uneventful. The nights were more interesting as Lolita caught up on the skills of being what she still called being vile, but no longer worried about.

They found themselves in thicker but still dry jungle as the land rose a bit, wherever the hell they were. Gaston stopped bitching about them being lost, now that it was becoming more obvious that they were. Gaston was prone to let the others figure things out for themselves.

But there were few complaints. They had plenty of water, ammo, and matches, so the food situation took care of itself, and, most important, they were still alive and out of the civil war.

They were camped at midday in a shady clearing, eating and waiting for the heat to ease off, when the picket posted at the north end of the break camp ran in, calling, "Captain Gringo! Someone comes! Someone comes singing strange songs!"

Captain Gringo leaped up from the log he'd been sharing with Lolita and ran to the perimeter and set-up machine gun. As he dropped behind the Maxim and armed it, Gaston flopped beside him, cocked his head, and observed, "I hear it. It does sound like singing. Not Spanish, though."

Captain Gringo told him to shut up as he listened in silence long enough to make out the sounds of at least a dozen men, singing in a ragged chorus:

"I belong to Glasgow, good old Glasgow town,
But there's something the matter wi' Glasgow,
For it's going around and around!
I'm only a simple working mon, as anyone here can see,
But when I've had a couple of drinks of a Saturday
Glasgow belongs to me!"

The two soldiers of fortune exchanged glances. Gaston said, "I do not think that is the sort of marching song either Nicaraguan army would sing."

Captain Gringo said, "You're right. It's a marching song or a marching outfit, though. Must be Brits. We've obviously overshot Greytown, as I feared, if they're singing about Glasgow to the north of us."

"Ay, laddie, as they say in Glasgow. Whoever they are, they are coming our way, non?"

"You're still right. Do we fade away like good little Indians or do we stay and challenge them?"

"Merde alors, either course could get us into the creek of merde sans paddle! Obviously, they are not lost, while we are. If we duck them, we remain lost!"

"That part was easy. What if they say something silly about arresting us?"

"Merde alors, on what charge? We are not trespassing on British Treaty territory. Wherever we are, it has to be Nicaragua. So they are the one's hunting without a license, non?"

"Hmm, that does give us a point to parley."

"That and this adorable machine gun. I vote we hail them and feed them the usual shit of the bull until we at least know where we are."

So they did.

The two soldiers of fortune watched from cover as a full platoon of thirty-odd marched into view as if they owned the jungle and everything else within a week's forced march. They were dressed in the khaki tropical battle kit of British infantry or constabulary, from pith helmets to hobnailed boots. Each man carried a bayonetted Martini slung over the same right shoulder. The officer in command out front got along in the world with only his swagger stick and Sam Browne pistol belt to carry. The others wore full field packs but seemed too well legged to stagger under the heavy loads, despite the heat and humidity. They were marching, of course, during the siesta hour when even the sensible Central American flies found a shady place to knock off for a while.

Gaston marveled, "No point man. No flank scouts. Do they think they are on *parade*?"

Captain Gringo said, "Let's find out what they think," as he snapped the arming lever of the Maxim for their edification and called out, "Halt! Who goes there?"

The officer out front held up his hand to halt his column, but came forward at a casual strut to call back, "Who goes there? Why, dash it all, old man, what do we look like, the ruddy Bulgarian navy?"

"Stop right there, lieutenant. If you'll look closer, you'll see this looks like a machine gun, and it's trained on you."

The officer stopped, frowning out from under the brim of his high-crowned helmet as he sputtered, "How dare you point a gun at us, whoever you are! We're on Her Majesty's business! I say, you can't be dagos if you're speaking English without garlic on your breath, what?"

"Never mind who we are. You're on Nicaraguan territory,

lieutenant. You don't look very Latin to us, either. What's the pitch?''

"Pitch? Pitch? I say, we hardly came into this perishing jungle for a game of cricket, what? We're Royal Constabulary. Searching for bandits, guerrillas, whatever you call those chaps. They shot up one of our outposts the other night. Actually broke some windows before they were beaten off. I say, you chaps aren't bandits, are you? Can't be the lot we were trailing. Lost their perishing trail up the cuesta a ways. They headed north after trying to raid us for supplies. Can't for the life of me think where they might have gone to. Nothing on either side but ruddy great swamps!''

Captain Gringo laughed and said, "I think we might have met them a while back. Don't worry about them anymore.''

"Why not? Can't have chaps like that lurking about a medical mission. Oh, I see, machine gun and all that, eh? I say, jolly good show, whoever you are.''

He waited, got no answer, and called out, "Oh, I say, you really should tell us who you are, you know.''

"Why? Are we on British territory?''

The officer had to think about that. He sighed and said, "See here, old chap, you sound like a Yank. Surely we're not going to quibble about the exact boundaries of the protectorate, are we? No bloody dago government of any sort within a day's march of here, and I can't say much for such government as they have in *any* part of this mucky place.''

He'd started forward again, without being invited. Captain Gringo let him. The simp seemed harmless, as long as his more serious troopers kept their distance. His flapped revolver holster was neatly closed. As he got within more comfortable talking range, they could see he was about thirty, with a florid face and toothbrush mustache. Like his hair peeking from under his topee, the mustache was a sort of spiderweb shade of nothing much. Perrito and old Julio had moved forward into view by now. The Brit frowned at them and asked Captain Gringo, "I say, are those dagos?"

"When you're right you're right. But it's more polite to call 'em Nicaraguans. This *is* Nicaragua, you know."

"Ah, I begin to see the light. You chaps are obviously soldiers of fortune. Leading your little brown brothers for one side or the other in this grotesque abuse of democratic process they use in place of elections down here. Don't tell me which side you're fighting for. It's none of our business, as long as you're not raiding British outposts. You wouldn't do a thing like that, would you?"

Captain Gringo laughed and said, "No. We have enough to worry about. Are you guys from Greytown? By the way, where the hell *is* Greytown from here?"

The officer waved vaguely to the northeast, over his shoulder, and said, "Over that way, I think. We're not stationed in the protectorate port itself. As I said, we're patrolling for a combined constabulary and medical mission, more or less directly behind you. I say, you seem to be barring our path home. You do mean to let us through, don't you?"

"Hold your horses, lieutenant. Got a few more questions. What's a British outpost doing this deep in Nicaraguan territory? We have to be miles inland from the coast."

"I suppose we are. I don't decide such matters. Whitehall in London says where we set up shop, what?"

"Yeah, on British territory. I didn't know London had jurisdiction over all of Nicaragua, lieutenant."

"What? What? All of Nicaragua? Good Lord, wouldn't take the bloody country as a gift! We're only here to protect the poor Mosquito Indians. Bloody dagos were popping them off like flies for no reason at all. We moved in at the request of the tribal leaders themselves. Told you Yanks we had to do it. President Cleveland doesn't seem to mind, actually."

"Well, he lives in Washington. No need to ask *Nicaragua's* permission, huh?"

"Good Lord, what a strange idea! You obviously seem to be involved in the current civil war down here. But since we're speaking English let's be honest. You know nobody is ever in charge of this country long enough to sign a treaty with anyone. We're just here to keep order on this part of the Mosquito Coast."

"You mean the part commanding approaches to the Rio San Juan and any future canal to the Pacific if the Panama deal falls through, right?"

"Ah, you do have a grasp of political reality after all, I see. But I say, why are we having such a long conversation about the simple facts of life? We're on our way back to our outpost. If you've any questions to ask, why not tag along and discuss them with our commandant? I'm sure you'd be welcome. White men stick together and all that?"

Captain Gringo laughed and said, "We'll stand aside and let you through. We'll pass on the invitation to visit your post, if it's all the same to you."

"Suit yourself, old boy. But I'm missing something. Surely you don't mean to suggest we can't be trusted to behave like gentlemen? Why, dash it all, had we meant you harm, you'd have jolly well known it by now."

"Oh yeah? Seems to me you're the guy I've got the drop on, pal."

"Rubbish. Just being civil is all. Could have taken you anytime. Just wanted to avoid needless unpleasantness, what?"

The two soldiers of fortune exchanged amused glances. Gaston said, "Perhaps we are missing something, m'sieur lieutenant. As a professional courtesy, would you mind telling us how you would have overwhelmed us with your gallant and no doubt partially sunstruck troops over there?"

The Britisher shrugged, said, "Oh, very well," and in a louder voice called out, "Sergeants Proctor and Muldoon!"

A voice to their left called out, "Sir!" from the jungle as

another from the far side called out the same way. The two soldiers looked to their right and saw a line of impassive, khaki-clad figures covering them from the flank. They looked the other way and saw the same thing. The patrols had them in a neat cross fire, although they still held their rifles politely at port arms.

Captain Gringo got wearily to his feet and said grudgingly, "You guys are better than I thought, lieutenant."

The officer shrugged and said, "I don't see why you shouldn't have thought we were good, Yank. Anyone could see at a glance we were the Royal Constabulary, what?"

As they tagged along with the Brits, the officer identified himself as Lieutenant Andrew MacLean. That, despite the Oxford accent, explained the marching song. As they marched with him he explained how he'd suckered them by having his flank patrols well out and moving Apache while the main column sang about Glasgow. He said they used that all the time in "Inja" and it always seemed to work.

They didn't have to explain why they went along with him. The Brits had made the point that if they'd been out to hurt anyone, the escapees would all be thoroughly shot up by now, and Captain Gringo needed basics like a compass and a map before they got in any more scrapes. They had a little money between them, and MacLean said there was a well-stocked trading post at the British base ahead.

Gaston had a suspicious nature. So he naturally tested the water a few times by suggesting in front of the officer that they might not have time to pass the time of day with his commandant at the outpost. MacLean didn't seem to care one way or the other. So they decided to chance it.

They arrived at the complex near sundown. It was bigger than they'd expected. The combined constabulary post, medical mission, trading post, and associated quarters was built around a modest parade ground and surrounded by a substantial parapet with squat towers of the same rough coral-block

masonry at all four corners. Guards patrolled the parapets
between the towers, and Captain Gringo spotted the muzzle
of his Maxim's twin peering out of the embrasures of the
nearest tower. When he asked MacLean if they were expecting
a siege, the Brit said, "Pays to be careful, what? Perishing
country is infested with all sorts of savages. Some of the
Indians can get a bit wild, too."

They filed inside with the khaki-clad troops, the escapees looking not a little nervous about it. But nobody tried
to disarm them, and one of the noncoms who spoke a little
Spanish took charge to lead the rest of the band to a part
of the compound where they could rest while Captain
Gringo and Gaston followed MacLean into the headquarters building.

Inside, they were introduced to an older man who looked
like a walrus and spoke even harder Oxford to follow than
MacLean's. He wore the crowns of a British major on his
khaki tunic and told them to call him Major Chalmers. So
they did.

Like MacLean, Chalmers seemed to have more important
things on his mind than who or what his visitors might be up
to, as long as they weren't aiming at *him*. He said the
political situation in Nicaragua was disgusting, which was
true enough, and though he offered them brandy and the first
cigars they'd had in some time, he seemed disinterested as
Captain Gringo fed him a line of bullshit about leading a
counterguerrilla group for the Granada faction. He'd picked
Granada because Granada was closer than León and hence
plausible.

Chalmers cut him off in mid-yarn with a wave of his
hand and a "Yes, yes, I'm sure you chaps know what
you're doing. We're not in the war zone here, fortunately.
Our current problems are, forgive me, more pressing to
the crown at the moment than the interminable Nicaraguan
mess."

He turned to MacLean and said, "If you say these chaps did a job on those ladrónes, so much for that matter. We'll of course treat them to such supplies as they need before they go on their way. What's the situation with those weird sisters over the other way? Have you located their bloody temple or whatever, yet?"

MacLean said, "Some of our Mosquito Indians have the old Jesuit mission pinpointed, sir. It's a good day's march inland. The sticky part is the perishing map."

"Map? Map? Bloody mission's not *on* our map, young sir!"

MacLean moved to a wall map over the nicely stocked sideboard and put a finger to it, saying, "It's about here, sir. Not on British ordnance maps, but unfortunately surveyed by the so-called local government, what?"

Chalmers said, "Make a *mark* there, man! Think I've a bloody memory for invisible fingerprints? That's better. What's the problem? I see no problem. Send a combat patrol out and level the bloody pest hole, what?"

MacLean shook his head and said, "Not without an international incident Whitehall would have to approve, major. It's not the bloody dagos I'm worried about. They're always moaning about something. But, as you see, the old mission's ruddy close to the Vanderbilt sphere of influence."

"Vanderbilt? Vanderbilt? Piffle! That old Yankee pirate has been dead some time, what?"

"He has, sir. But the Yanks are still interested in everything that close to the Vanderbilt Trust's transport net, land holdings, bananas, and whatever. Could lead to a bit of a row if uninformed British constabulary were seen shooting up natives that far from the coast."

Chalmers looked unhappy, took a healthy swig of brandy, and said, "Have to do something about those bloody cultists. They're bothering our Indians. Beastly difficult to keep an

Indian in pants and church with those ruddy Sisters of Santaria frightening them with black magic."

Gaston had been listening with interest. He said, "Forgive me, m'sieur le major, but I am missing something. You say there is a Jesuit mission over to the west? But the Spanish colonial authorities expelled the Jesuit order years ago. They had a most unfortunate habit of standing up for Indian rights and opposing chattel slavery, so naturally they had to go. So far, none of the revolutionary governments down here has seen fit to invite the Jesuits back. Their glorious new constitutions neglected to get rid of the old Spanish tax laws, either."

Chalmers nodded and said grudgingly, "Quite so. I see you do know your way about down here, Lieutenant Verrier. The mission under discussion is no longer run by the Jesuits. It was taken over some time ago by the so-called order of the Sisters of Santaria. Weren't you paying attention?"

"I was, m'sieur, and while I must confess to being at most a deathbed Catholic, there is no such order as the Sisters of Santaria. I may not know my nuns. I find them très boring, as a matter of fact. But I know my saints, or the ones my less intelligent relatives prayed to. There is no Catholic Saint Ria. Rita, oui. But Ria is not a name. It's a tidal estuary in Spanish and nothing at all in French."

Major Chalmers shrugged and looked bored as MacLean explained, "They're not real nuns at all, what? Santaria is some sort of dago cult. Mishmash of primitive Christianity and voodoo, macumba, or whatever you want to call that business the niggers do with drums and chicken feathers, eh what?"

Gaston said, "Ah, one begins to see the light. Pray continue, m'sieur."

Major Chalmers frowned at Gaston and said, "What? Continue? Piffle! Nothing to do but wait until we get permission from our government. Can't risk an international flap just to save some perishing Indians, what?"

MacLean, who'd already shown that he was brighter than he looked, said, "Begging the major's pardon. Those bloody cultists practice human sacrifice! Leaving that aside, they've been blackmailing the coastal chiefs to denounce the protectorate. It may work, too. The old Mosquito king who signed the original agreement with us is long dead. If the Indians themselves ask us to pull out . . . well, you know how tiresome the Yanks can be about that Monroe business. Her Majesty wouldn't have a leg to stand on if the natives, as well as the so-called Nicaraguan government, agreed we have no business here!"

Chalmers looked even unhappier, but said, "Can't do anything about it tonight. Take at least a week for those fuddy-duddies in London to even find us on the map, and some idiot is sure to raise the issue of Catholic persecution. Elizabeth never should have cut off Mary Stuart's head like that. But she did, and those tarted-up Sisters of Santaria do look like nuns, to an Anglican at least. Doubt the Pope would approve of 'em, if he even knew they existed. Sisters of Santaria, my Aunt Fanny Adams! Ruddy lot of pagan whores in real nuns' costumes. Can't stand papists, myself. But I must say I've never heard of any Catholic order carving people up with stone knives, eh what?"

"They have to be put out of business," said MacLean, flatly.

Chalmers said, "Right. We'll discuss the matter when and if we get the go-ahead from Whitehall. Let's get to the business these rather adventurous chaps have with us, MacLean."

He turned back to the soldiers of fortune as if relieved to have a problem Whitehall didn't have to approve, and asked, "How can we be of service to you and your lot, Captain Walker? Owe you for dealing with those bandits for us, what?"

Captain Gringo smiled and said, "That's very kind of you, sir. I have only a few modest favors to ask. As MacLean here can tell you, we seem to have picked up too many female, ah, war refugees along the way. With your permission, we'd like to escort them into Greytown, where they'd be safe. Naturally, my men and I would leave them there and return to the war zone to serve the Granada cause.''

"I see. No problem. We have a steam launch coming up the river from the coast once a week, if you'd like to hang about. Otherwise, you could march to Greytown in a day or so. We can provide you with supplies, if you need 'em, what?''

"Thank you, major, we do. I'll pay for the gun oil and rations MacLean here says we can pick up at the trading post. Some ground cloths and blankets would come in handy too. But let *us* worry about supplies, if we have your permission to move our innocent bystanders into British Greytown.''

"Quite so. Already said you didn't need my blessings. We're not out here to check the papers of passing strangers. Naturally you have some sort of commissions or whatever to show the authorities in Greytown?''

The two soldiers of fortune exchanged glances but managed to hide their dismay. Captain Gringo smiled as if he had something to smile about and said, "Ah, actually we lost our commissions and orders when those bandits we told you about shot us up in the swamp.''

Chalmers blinked owlishly and said, "What? What? No proper papers and you're mucking about with all those rifles and a machine gun?''

"Well, you said yourself things are run sort of informally down here, major. I'm sure Granada will issue us all the new documentation we need when we get back from our counter-guerrilla sweep. But meanwhile, those noncombatants are slowing us down. Couldn't we just explain to the guys in Greytown when we get there?''

The major glanced up at the lieutenant. MacLean shook his head and said, "Not bloody likely, what? Perishing navy base, and, well, we all know the bloody R.N. Probably hold you chaps until they could verify your commissions with one side or the other. Might even intern you for the duration. Her Majesty never gave permission for a civil war so close to her sphere of influence, what?''

Gaston laughed, easily, considering, and said, "One does not look forward with enthusiasm to being interned for the duration of a war down here! The current one's been going on for generations! All in all, I think perhaps we shall just be on our way. What do you think, Dick?''

"I'm with you. Dragging those refugees all the way back to Granada will be a drag indeed, but you heard what the man said.''

MacLean had been thinking. As Captain Gringo started to rise, the junior officer said, "Wait. Let's have another drink and talk about this impasse. We do owe you, after all, what?''

As MacLean poured, the major said, "Am I supposed to be in the dark, too, young sir? Out with it, man! I can see you've something devious on your fey Celtic mind, eh what?''

MacLean passed out the drinks as he said, "It occurred to me, sir, that we could issue these gentlemen a safe conduct to and from Greytown.''

"On what grounds?'' asked Chalmers, looking unconvinced in advance and adding, ''You heard them say they're soldiers of fortune working for the side that *The Times* say will lose! How in bloody hell can the British Constabulary issue papers to people working for another bloody government? My God, it sounds like something the *Yanks* would do!''

MacLean chuckled dryly and said, "I see you've been watching developments in the Panama area, sir. Nicaragua would be a crown colony today if old Commodore Vanderbilt hadn't outfoxed a lot of people with his, ah, informal approach to power politics.''

"Good God, not Vanderbilt again, MacLean. I tell you, the blighter is dead! Get to the *point*, young sir!"

MacLean said, "We could issue anyone anything, if they were on Her Majesty's business, sir."

Chalmers sipped his brandy and said, "True, true, but these chaps are fighting for some perishing Nicaraguan warlord!"

"They could take a detour, sir. What if these gentlemen and their guerrillas could be persuaded to handle that Santaria mess for us? Please don't yell at me until I've finished, sir. My plan is simple. I'll bet our guests have already grasped it in its entirety, what?"

Chalmers sighed and said, "I wish someone would explain it to me, then!"

Gaston did. He said, "I see the light, m'sieur le major. What this très Byzantine young officer suggests is that we, irregulars in no way connected with the British military, have certain freedoms to act in ways that could otherwise cause flappings in Washington and who knows where, if anyone could blame it on your adorable majesty."

He turned to Captain Gringo and asked, "What do you think, Dick? Would you like to visit a convent with me?"

Captain Gringo grimaced and said, "The major's right. It's weird, and I haven't even seen it yet. What's the catch, MacLean?"

MacLean looked blank and asked, "What catch are we talking about? It's a simple enough proposition. You scratch our backs. We scratch yours, eh what?"

"Your talking about scratching said somebody with a machine gun. What if we get in trouble and need Her Majesty to bail us out?"

MacLean shook his head and said, "Don't get in trouble. We'll have never heard of you if you do. If we wanted to involve Britain in the mess at all, we'd have sent out patrols and simply cleaned those cultists out long ago. We can issue you more ammo. We can issue you most anything. If you make it back, with the job well done, and no repercussions we'd never be able to explain . . .''

"Gotcha," Captain Gringo cut in, adding, "It's a shitty deal, but it's the only deal in town. Let's cut the deck. Up front, if we wipe out or disperse those cultists bothering your native charges, we get what for openers?''

MacLean didn't consult his superior as he said, flatly and with no Oxford bullshit, "Safe-conduct passes to or from all points in the British Mosquito Coast protectorate, to use as you see fit. Period.''

"No cash?''

"I said *period*. We haven't any cash to give you, save for petty trading-post transactions nobody in Whitehall will ever question. Would it save time if I stated plainly that I don't buy your story about working for anybody but yourselves, and that I've a pretty good idea why you need those papers, Walker?''

"Yeah, it would. Gaston's right about you being a pretty Byzantine guy on a chessboard. Okay, ask us no questions and we'll tell you no more lies. We have a deal on the papers. Do we get 'em before or after?''

"Surely you jest?''

"Hey, does it hurt to ask? How do we know you won't double-cross us? Where is it signed in blood that we get safe-conduct papers after we pull your chestnuts out of the jungle, MacLean?''

MacLean sipped his own brandy and just raised an eyebrow. Captain Gringo nodded and said, "Right. Once we massacre a bunch of natives for you, the sooner you send us on our way, the better. Are these so-called Sisters of Santaria *all* dames, by the way?''

MacLean shook his head and said, "Only a handful of voodoo ladies running the old Jesuit mission as cult headquarters. Most of the cultists are male, and believe me, when you see them you won't feel hesitant about fighting them!''

Major Chalmers muttered, "Ruddy bunch of cannibals, what?" and lowered his head to the blotter on his desk to sleep it off.

Gaston asked, "How many men can we take with us?"

MacLean retorted, "How many have you got that are good in a fight? I suggest you leave anyone who's not, here with the women. We can give you a handful of Indian guides. They'll have machetes. That's it. We don't arm unreliable natives, and if the Mosquitoes were reliable we wouldn't have this problem to deal with."

Captain Gringo counted in his head. He did it again and still didn't like it. He asked, "How many fighting men on the other side?"

MacLean said, "We don't know. Just found out where the blighters were, for God's sake. Could be a few dozen. Could be as many as a hundred or more in and about the old mission. Take the old mission out and that should put an end to the business. The mother superior is supposed to be immortal and invincible. Prove *that* a superstition and the whole house of cards falls apart, what ho?"

"If you say so. You say we could run up against as many as a hundred-plus we have to convert the hard way?"

"We'll give you extra machine-gun ammo."

"Gee, thanks! Run that shit about immortal mother superiors by us again."

MacLean shrugged and replied, "There's only one. The other so-called nuns are allowed to die once in a while, it seems. We don't know much about the head witch of the operation. If any constable had ever seen her he'd have arrested her, naturally. The native superstition is that she's ever young, ever beautiful, and has all sorts of occult powers."

"So she's what, thirty, forty, a hundred?"

MacLean shook his head and said, "At least a couple of hundred years old, according to the Indians."

Gaston snorted in derision and said, "She must have a très fantastique cosmetic set, non?"

MacLean didn't answer. He could see Captain Gringo had something more important to say.

The tall American did. He said, "Okay. Anyone can wear a mask or decant a new broad into an old costume. What are these supposed occult powers she's supposed to wield, MacLean?"

The Brit replied, "Dash it all, chaps, how on earth are we supposed to know? We've never *seen* any of the weird sisters. They're just out there in the jungle, mucking up the heads of our bloody Indians!"

He was going Oxford again, so Captain Gringo knew he'd told them all he thought they needed to know. He stood up and said, "It's dark out. We can't do anything right now and I have to sleep on your proposition. One last question. Could we send the women on into Greytown with a couple of the older guys?"

MacLean shook his head, smiled boyishly, and said, "If you did that, you'd have no reason to go to Greytown yourselves, eh what?"

"Right, and you'd have no way of making sure we came back. You're a pretty slick guy, MacLean."

"Thank you, Captain Gringo. Coming from you, that's a compliment."

The tall American shot a wary glance at the drunken major and asked quietly, "Does he know?"

MacLean shook his head and said, "No. He'd never go along with my plan to fight fire with fire."

"Gotcha. You knew all along, right?"

"Not until one of my men overheard one of your gang mention it. But not to worry. I'd never have picked you for this mission had I not known who you were. It's a job for hired killers, and they tell us you're the best in the business!"

Captain Gringo growled, "Thanks, I think. What's our leverage against you turning us in for the rewards on our heads, which you have to know about, once we've done your dirty work for you?''

MacLean shook his head and said, ''That would be stupid of us. Once you wipe that cult out, we'll never want you discussing it in open court at an extradition hearing in Greytown, eh what?''

Gaston sighed and said, ''He has us by the short hairs, Dick. But, on the other hand, it seems pratique that the British constabulary would not wish the world to know they made a deal with a pair of wanted men, non?''

Captain Gringo looked at MacLean as he said, ''Maybe. What happens if we blow it, MacLean?''

McLean said flatly, ''Don't. It would be my duty to the crown to turn you in as not only wanted but rather useless criminals.''

When MacLean's Sergeant Muldoon escorted the two soldiers of fortune to where the others had been allowed to set up camp, they found their followers in better shape than in recent memory. The campsite was in a semipatio formed by wings of the day school for Indian kids and the base hospital. The windows of the school were dark because, Muldoon explained, the perishing natives were not allowed inside the walls after dark. The curtained windows of the hospital shed soft steady light on the subject because someone always had yellow jack and the ward lamps stayed on all night to keep the nursing sisters from tripping over bedpans.

Without being asked, the Brits had issued ground cloths and cotton flannel blankets and had broken out field rations and some cooking utensils for their guests. Muldoon apologized for the lack of a roof, explaining, ''Our own quarters are cramped, you see, sors. The post has just been built and, faith, it was never designed with hotel accommodations in mind.''

Gaston frowned at the heavy coral masonry of the nearest stretch of outer defenses and cocked an eyebrow. Muldoon caught his meaning and said, "Spanish. The walls themselves was left to us by some long dead don. When we marched in, it was just an imposing ruin. As you see, sor, British engineers can do wonders with milled lumber and tin roofing.''

They didn't argue the point. So Muldoon left and they squatted down by the women around the fire to see what was cooking as the men crowded in to find out what the powwow in G.H.Q. had been about.

Captain Gringo knew bad news felt better on a full stomach. So he announced a council of war after coffee and dessert. The fat girl, Gordita, seemed to be in charge of the big cannibal pot she was stirring. He put a vile hand under Lolita's skirt to comfort her and keep her quiet as he asked Gordita what she was making.

Gordita sighed, wiped her free hand across her greasy face, and said, "It would be a grand guisado if they'd issued me a few pounds of chocolate. Alas, all I had to work with was beans, rice, salt pork, and canned beef."

"*I* put on the coffeepot!" said Lolita proudly, reaching down to pull his wrist closer to home plate.

He didn't really want to finger fuck his adelita in mixed company. He thought Gordita was overimaginative, too. He asked the fat girl, "No offense, Gordita, but you were going to put *chocolate* in that stew?"

She said, "Sí, I cook everything with chocolate. Haven't you ever had chicken molena?"

"Okay, chocolate-dipped chicken is only a *little* weird. But, Jesus, mixed with bully beef . . . ?"

She shrugged and said, "It is true some people do not like chocolate as much as me. At home I worked in a bakery, where I could get all I wanted. I have not had any chocolate since those terrible soldados arrested us all. The craving was killing me for the first twenty-four hours. But now I may survive until I can buy more chocolate. Will there be chocolate in Greytown? The Anglos who gave me this food for to cook said they do not eat as much chocolate as we do.''

He grunted, ''Nobody does. You ought to kick the habit, Gordita. Your skin is already starting to clear up. But that's your problem. If that stew is boiled soft enough to cut with an ax, let's eat. I'm hungry as the devil!''

Lolita moved her hot little love box closer to his invisible hand as she agreed she, too, had hungers beyond belief. He pulled his hand out to eat with before he had to wash it.

Gordita was a good cook, even without chocolate to throw in everything. Left with earthly ingredients, the fat girl had seasoned her big pot of guisado just right and the results stuck to the ribs and didn't promise to repeat later on. Lolita's coffee was good, too. Or, in truth, maybe one's first square meal in days always felt like dining at the Ritz.

The others were as hungry, of course, so the pot soon was empty. Only Gordita complained they hadn't issued enough rations for third helpings. One of the other women broke open a box of cheap but welcome cheroots the constabulary had issued. So as the men smoked to one side and let the women police up the camp, all seemed right with the world for a change.

Captain Gringo decided that now was as good a time as any to give them the news about the British deal. As he filled them in he saw more than one man make the sign of the cross. Most of them had never heard of the Sisters of Santaria. Those who had, of course, had opposing opinions. Old Julio said he'd heard about them and that they were indeed pagans who indulged in black magic, human sacrifice, and other scary stuff. Perrito shook his head and said that while he'd never been anywhere near the mission, some Indians he'd met in his travels had told him it was a real

Catholic mission, only better. Regular medical missionaries couldn't cure consumption or the great pox. The Sisters of Santaria could cure anything and, if they *really* liked you, raise you from the dead.

Captain Gringo raised a hand to nip the argument in the bud and say, "Either way, the Brits want us to clean them out. I'm not enthused about shooting nuns, real or not. We could probably defrock them, chase them away, or whatever, without roughing them up too bad. Their male cult followers are another story. MacLean said they outnumber us more than ten to one, and he was trying to *sell* us the deal. Any suggestions, muchachos?"

Gaston said, "Oui, let us cross the British double and simply scamper into the jungle again."

There was a chorus of agreement. Captain Gringo said, "Shut up, Gaston. You're not a muchacho. You're a dirty old man." He turned back to the others to explain, "That was the first idea I had. We could just take the supplies and run. The major is dead drunk and MacLean was working on it. I don't know if those guards up on the walls have orders about us or not. We could still slip out of here without much fuss, given a stab in the back here and there. But where does that leave us?"

Gaston said, "Off and running with supplies we did not have this afternoon, hein?"

Captain Gringo nodded, but said, "Big deal. There's a telegraph line running east to the coast. Even if we cut it, we'd play hell strolling into Greytown with the colonial police force mad at us at one end and asking all sorts of foolish questions at the other. The whole point was to get you guys, and, above all, the girls, to a safe place. Greytown's only safe if the Brits make nice-nice instead of boom-boom at us, see?"

Perrito asked, "What if we simply agree to the plan,

marched out to wipe out that old mission, and just kept marching?''

"Two unpleasant catches, Perrito. MacLean wants us to leave the women here. So that would be the last we'd ever see of them. Assuming you're all used to jacking off if need be, the second catch is that we'd be marching back into the war zone. We'd be idiots to leave our guns anywhere along the way because, aside from opposing armies, the war zone is infested with banditos, ladrónes, and just plain mean bastards of all shapes and sizes. But if we marched into an army, out of uniform and fully armed . . . Lots of luck!''

Julio said, "We could tell them we were on their side, whatever side they were on, no?''

Captain Gringo shook his head and said, "No. Those pricks who arrested us all were going to shoot us just for being unknown to them *before* we were packing guns. And remember, we don't even know whether they were for Granada or León! We're in the south, so most troops we run into should be Granadistas. But we could be making an awful mistake by shouting Viva Granada before we were in shooting range. Once we're close enough to an army to discuss politics with them, it probably wouldn't help.''

Perrito took a thoughtful draw on his smoke before he said, "There is still the border, no?''

"Yeah, that's a better chance to take than looking for an army to join. But it's not as safe as Greytown with safe-conduct papers. The Costa Ricans are reasonably sane, for down here. That's why Gaston and I hole up in San José between jobs. But Costa Rica has border guards and I don't think they want any guerrillas on either side crossing the San Juan to steal their women and rape their chickens. At best they'd arrest and disarm us. Then they'd either put us against the wall or boot our asses back across the border. You Nicaraguans make Costa Ricans nervous, no offense.''

He took a sip of coffee to give them time to think about the options.

Perrito was the savvy jungle runner of the bunch. He blew a thoughtful smoke ring and said, "I do not like shooting nuns, even if they are not nuns. But, all in all, it seems more complicated to double-cross the English than it does to simply go out and get the damned job over with!"

Tio Julio protested, "We are not soldados! Not real soldados, anyway. There are less than a dozen of us left. True, we have modern weapons and that marvelous machine gun, but Jesus, Maria, y José, those cultists outnumber us dozens to one, and they are forted behind stone walls! I vote we pass the mission by and throw ourselves on the mercy of the first Nicaraguan authorities we meet!"

Another man who'd been smoking quietly growled, "I don't. I have grown fond of my adelita. I wish for to come back to her and try some positions we may have missed in the safe surroundings of the British protectorate. As for throwing myself on anyone's mercy, I was already at the mercy of those motherfucking triple-thumbed toads in that cellar we escaped from, and I never wish for to spend a night like that again!"

Most of the resultant growls were in agreement. Captain Gringo said, "All right, muchachos. Sleep on the idea, and anyone who doesn't want to march with me in the morning can stay here with the women. I'm turning in. It looks like we've got a long day ahead of us no matter what we decide. Coming, Gaston?"

Gaston rose to follow him, saying, "Not yet, but the redhead has our new sleeping bag set up under the props of the empty schoolhouse. I never got to thank you for fixing me up like that, my unselfish adorable child. Merde alors, if she were even a shade more passionate, my poor back would be broken by now. I'm either getting old or she's getting younger every time we're alone."

"I'm so happy for you." Captain Gringo sighed, trying not to remember he'd seen Rubia first and that she was still the best-looking head in town. Knowing she was a great lay didn't make it any easier on him. But what the hell, he had some good stuff waiting for him, too.

As they walked the short distance together, Gaston murmured, "Listen, Dick, if you want any of that redhead, there's more than enough to go around. To tell the truth, there's more icing on the cake than a man of my delicate tastes prefers as a steady diet."

"My heart bleeds for you."

"Sacrebleu, you unfeeling monster, I need *help*! That manic redhead could take on the whole British constabulary and yell for more. Come to think of it, she probably will, as soon as we march out."

"Okay, so what's your problem? Take what you want and just turn over and go to sleep, right?"

"Wrong. I tried that. She keep waking me up, jerking my poor tired shaft. Are you sure you can't spell me half the night? That way we'd both get a few hours' sleep, non?"

Captain Gringo laughed and turned away to rejoin Lolita. Great minds ran in the same channels. The pretty little Mestiza and recent virgin had spread their bedding in the semidarkness under the frame schoolhouse, out of earshot and sight of Gaston and Rubia's appointed orgy. The sandy soil under the canvas ground cloth was dry. Lolita was already naked under the thin cotton flannel blanket. As he undressed to slide in beside her, Lolita said, "This is a marvelous place to be vile. There are few insects. Gordita left a nice smudge fire going, and I think those nice Anglos sprayed something under here, no?"

He sniffed and said, "Yeah, kerosene and citronella bug spray. They've probably sprayed oil on all the mosquito ponds for a mile or so around, too. When garrison troops run out of rocks to whitewash, they spray oil on all the puddles in sight. You and the other muchachas should be okay here until we get back.''

She didn't like that idea at all, even after he'd explained the deal. She held her nude curves close to his naked flesh as she sobbed, "For how can I be your adelita if I am not to march with you, Deek?''

He rolled her on her back, parted the lips of her love box with his suddenly inspired screw driver, and treated her as his adelita indeed for a while. But tonight his heart wasn't really in it, even though his pecker was. He was really too worried about the future to enjoy the present as much as he would have if this had been a hotel in San José. Lolita took his distracted and hence protracted lovemaking as a compliment. Her less complicated views on life allowed her to enjoy the here and now just swell. He envied her, in a way, as he let her get on top to bounce as happily as a little kid riding a merry-go-round. There was much to be said for the peon view of life. The only trouble with living out each day to the hilt and letting mañana take care of itself was that mañana always came, and folks who never planned ahead tended to die younger than they might have planned, if they'd planned at all.

He smiled fondly up at her pretty face and bouncing bare breasts as she did all the work with considerable skill, considering what her mother had always told her. She threw back her head, arched her spine, and tingled on his shaft in orgasm before falling limply down in his welcoming arms and sighing, "Oh, that felt so nice and vile. Were you vile in me, just now, Deek? Forgive me, I was enjoying myself too much to pay full attention.''

He patted her back and said, "It felt vile as hell.'' He knew she'd want more in a minute, and in his oddly detached mood he could wait. Meanwhile, the contractions on his semierection sure felt better than pissing.

She nibbled his collar bone and asked, "For why were you

smiling so at me just now, Deek? Do you think I do it funny?''

"You do it just the way I like it. I was just thinking about a story. The one about the ant and the grasshopper.''

"I don't know that one. Do I make love like an ant or a grasshopper? I confess I have no intention of ever trying either one. That would *really* be vile, no?''

"It wouldn't even work. You're not *that* tight. But yeah, you do move sort of like a grasshopper. Tonight, for some reason, I feel more like the wise old ant. But I'll be damned if I can find the hole I'd like to crawl into for the coming winter!''

She started to move her hips experimentally, with her knees tucked under his armpits. She said, "If I am to play grasshopper, your reed should stand a little straighter, querido. Are you tired of me already? My mother said men tire all too soon of women.''

It would have been cruel to tell her her mother was right. He felt guilty as hell, but in truth, once you'd had a sweet brainless dame in all the positions that didn't hurt, what was all the fuss about?

He tried to inspire himself by thinking of other women. The ones that gave him a hard-on just to think about when he was down on his luck and alone in the sack. That actress, Ellen Terry, was so beautiful in the *Police Gazette* that young guys were jerking off over her all over the world tonight. Could it feel any different inside Ellen Terry's snatch? Dammit, he was in a pussy so fresh that it seemed a violation of the pure-food laws to come in it. So why the hell was his pecker at half-mast?

He knew she needed at least a couple of more orgasms before she'd fall asleep. And if she didn't fall asleep she'd want to talk all night. He didn't want to talk, even to a bedmate with something interesting to say. He had a lot on his mind and he wanted to think.

She murmured, "You are so quiet, querido. Are you angry about something?"

He was pissed off about a lot of things. But she wasn't one of them. So he kissed her, rolled her on her back, and started kissing her all over as he played her body like a piano with his hands. She giggled and said, "Oh, that tickles so nicely. But just what do you have in mind, querido? You seem to be kissing me and touching me all over at once. Can't you make up your mind which part you wish for to use and abuse the most?"

He started kissing his way down her brown belly as he fondled her naked breasts. They were the shape and size of ripe eggplants. As he tongued her belly just above her pubic hair, Lolita spread her thighs but protested, "Oh, no! My mother said girls who let men do *that* could wind up in insane asylums!"

That sounded fair. Seafood could be distasteful in a warm climate where few women showered regularly. But he had to do *something* to her, and what the hell, nobody else but him had ever been in there.

Once he got used to the not-too-bad smell, he had it half-licked. As he started teasing her clit with his tongue and fingering the depths under it, Lolita raised her buttocks clear of the canvas with her strong brown limbs and hissed, "Oh, my God! My mother was crazy!"

He got a knee on either side of her with his groin above her upper story as he proceeded seriously to swab out her cellar for her. She moaned and reached up to clutch his dangling dong. But while most would have known what in the hell to do with it by now, the foolish girl just kept playing with it like it was a damned doll. It was hard as need be now. So he spoke into her pink telephone, hissing, "Do it to me, dammit!"

She protested, "Oh, I couldn't! It's too big and vile. I'm sure it would make me feel sick to my stomach and . . . Oh, more, more, more! Put all four fingers in and suck harder on whatever in God's name feels so *good* down there!''

He lowered his hips to get his erection between her big breasts. She caught on and thrust them together around him with her hands as he started moving. Thanks to not having bathed all day and the early start she had on him, her firm breasts were just oily enough to slide in and out between without chafing. It felt more unusual than really good. But now that he was this hot, he could have come in a barrel bung, so what the hell.

She giggled and raised her head to get a better view of his posterior as he ate her and screwed her tits. She strained her neck and stuck out an experimental tongue to tickle his bounding scrotum just below his rectum. It drove him to greater effort. The results were driving her nuts, too. She said, ''Oh, you taste nice and salty, querido. I think I am almost there and, oh, sí, sí, let *me* be wicked, too!''

He raised his hips and moved back as her contractions on his sex-slicked fingers announced she was coming. He deliberately slowed to keep her right on the very edge. It was easier with parts of himself that couldn't come, themselves. She moaned, grabbed his erection tightly in one hand, then kissed it, hesitated, and slid it into the pursed-lipped wetness of her little mouth. He started moving it to show her what he wanted. Lolita was a willing pupil and a fast study. She proceeded to give him a blow job that would have cost twenty dollars in Dodge City as she slowly relaxed her hand on the shaft to take more and more as she got used to the idea. She got used to it just great as she shuddered in protracted orgasm with four fingers in her to the knuckles. She got the tip past her gagging point, removed her hand, and swallowed it to the root to let him come deep in her throat, as he returned the favor by rotating his fingertips on her uterus as she clamped down on his knuckles harder than most men shook hands.

As he rolled off to lie on his back, panting for his second

wind, Lolita stared in wonder up at the boards just above them and swallowed a few more times to settle her digestion before she mused, "I suppose I will end my days in some insane asylum. But, all in all, I think it's worth it!"

He put a casual hand on her warm brown belly and said, "Yeah, we'd better not try that every night. It does tend to drive one ga-ga."

"I *like* going ga-ga with you, Deek, and in the morning you are leaving for who knows how long? Now that we have been vile at both ends, is there anything left we haven't tried? I wish to be able to say my soldado and me have done everything that men and women can do to one another."

He said, "Not to the other women, I hope." Then since they were laid but heads to each other's knees, anyway, he moved his hand, dipped it in to get it wet, and started fingering her anus, observing, "This is about the only place I haven't come in you, if you're up to fun and games."

She flinched and said, "Oh, I don't know, Deek. That hurts, a little, I think."

"You think? Don't you know?"

"I'm not sure. My mother said men who did that to women were beasts who would burn in hell. But it's your soul."

He grinned and eased one finger in. It made him sort of hot again to consider the possibilities of new fields to conquer. She was tight as a drum in there and her smooth rectal walls felt yummy. But even one finger seemed a little much in such a tight little ass. She hissed, "No deeper, por favor! I am sorry, Deek. I wish for to be totally depraved, now that I know what fun it is, but I don't think we could ever get that monstrous thing of yours in *there*! Even one finger is most uncomfortable, although rather interesting. Could you perhaps play with me back there with your fingers as we did it the more usual way?"

That sounded fair. So he remounted her, old-fashioned,

sort of. Few did it old-fashioned with the girl's ankles locked around the nape of the man's neck. He played with her back door as he went in and out the front for a while. But she was too tight and the sideshow was just distracting both of them. So he settled down just to screw her silly, and she must have liked it. After she'd come twice, ahead of him, she begged for mercy and let him stop.

He was willing enough. He'd taken the edge off his appetite without tiring himself too much for the morning march, he hoped. He reclined beside her, smoking a cheroot. In a little while she rolled over on her side with a contented little sigh and started snoring softly.

He finished the smoke, still wide awake. The compound was quiet. Thanks to the bug spray, not even a cricket was allowed to chirp within earshot. So, naturally, he heard it when a floorboard squeaked in the schoolhouse above.

He frowned thoughtfully. It was none of his business if someone wanted to prowl a deserted schoolroom at night. Or was it?

He quietly slipped on his pants, put the shoulder holster on over his bare skin, and eased away from the sleeping girl to see what there was to see, topside.

He assumed the doors would be locked. But he'd noticed the side windows were not glazed but only fitted with jalousy slat shutters. He stood looking around for a moment. Not a creature was stirring, and the smudge fire didn't cast enough light for anyone to see him from the walls above, even if anyone was looking. He found a window that wasn't completely shuttered, opened the jalousies, and hoisted himself up and over the sill to drop to one knee in a dark and hopefully deserted room.

As his eyes adjusted to the even dimmer light inside, Captain Gringo saw he was in a schoolroom that looked just like a schoolroom was supposed to look. Desks with built-in seats were bolted to the floor in neat rows. The teacher's desk was at the far end, in front of a slate board. Any English lessons the Indian kids had been getting had been neatly erased. In fact, the place looked spanking new and unused. Sergeant Muldoon had said they'd just set up shop here.

He heard something too big to be a mouse moving in the next room. He drew the .38 and eased in on the sound of someone opening and shutting drawers. He caught the red-head, red-handed as well, going through the desk drawers in the neighboring classroom.

He holstered the .38 and said, "Buenas noches, señorita. Find the apple for the teacher yet?"

Rubia nearly jumped out of her skin. Since she was stark naked, she didn't have far to go. She gasped, "Oh, it's you. I thought I'd been caught!"

He said, "You were, but I guess I don't take it as seriously as the constabulary might. What in the hell are you using for a brain, Rubia? This is a classroom, infested at best with primitive Indians who don't even own shoes. If you're going to take up burglary, at least bust into some corner bodega where you might manage to steal at least a banana."

She sat her bare rump on the edge of the larger teacher's desk, unaware or unashamed of her state of dishabille, and explained, "I am not a thief. I am simply curious. I have never been in an English school before. Do you suppose they could be *Protestants*?"

"Good guess. Queen Victoria is the official head of the Anglican Church. That's probably what makes her talk so stuffy. What were you looking for in the drawers, signs of heretic tendencies? The Pope and the archbishop of Canterbury haven't been spying on each other in ages. They divvied up the territory years ago, red."

"Not down here!" she said, adding, "It's not right to make Protestants of Nicaraguan Indians!"

"Look at it this way. All you religious Nicaraguans have ever done for the Mosquito Indians has been to treat them like mosquitoes. Don't worry your pretty head about it. Rice-bowl Christians of any variety tend to revert to their old tom-tom gods as soon as the missionary with said rice bowl turns his back on 'em."

She leaned back, bracing her imposing torso on her arms with hands flat on the desk behind her as she smiled in the dim light and asked, "Do you really think I'm pretty, Deek? You have an odd way of showing a woman you admire her!"

He ran his eyes up and down her naked curves as he grinned and said, "You sure offer lots of admiration for full inspection, red. I take it Gaston's turned in for the night?"

"Sí, he said something about wishing for to be rested up for the march ahead of him in the morning. Do you know what he did tonight instead of fucking me the right way?"

"Never mind. It was probably a smart move, and what the hell, you must have enjoyed it."

"Oh, I did. But a woman wishes a feeling of fullness in her when she comes. Would you like to fill my void, Deek? As you see, we are all alone, and you don't seem sleepy, either."

He said, "Well, I did miss out on one position tonight," and then, as she smiled lewdly and invitingly, he dropped his pants around his ankles and stepped out of them, in only his shoulder rig. His .38 had been put away until needed. His other weapon, to his mild surprise, seemed loaded and cocked.

She started to recline back across the desk as he moved in. He turned her around and bent her over the desk with her thighs braced against it and her derriere aimed up at him. Her hips were wider and her buttocks were paler than the ass he'd just played with. So the novelty inspired him to new heights as he spit on his fingers, lubricated the old ring-dang-do, and shoved it in position.

The redhead hissed, "Not there! You're too high, querido!" But he said, "I know where I'm going. You said you wanted to feel full, right?"

"Oh, no! I thought we settled that discussion of Greek the other night, and from what the others told me, I assumed you were only joking! I don't *want* it in me that way, Deek! I don't *like* to take it in my rear!"

He said, "Who asked what *you* liked?" and shoved in hard.

She gasped in dismay as he entered her that way and simply proceeded to cornhole her for his own pleasure. Captain Gringo was a gentle lover, to human beings, but Rubia was an animal with a mean streak, and anal rape was a novelty he couldn't try on any woman with half a heart.

She started beating on the desk with her fists as she groaned, "Take it out! For God's sake take it out! You're killing me!"

"Lie still then, if you're dead. What's the matter, babe? I thought you liked it hot and dirty?"

She started to cry. That made him feel a little guilty, but it felt even better in her as she began to get used to it and take it deep and fast.

She arched her back to help as she said, "All right, if you promise to put it in me right, once you've finished torturing me back there!"

"Is it still hurting? Hell, I thought you were a woman of experience."

"I am, but I told you I wasn't a *Greek* woman of experience, damn you! Are you almost finished?"

"Hardly. Just getting my second wind. Just relax and enjoy it, red."

"You're crazy! Who could enjoy being raped in the ass by

a horse? Uh, would you either take it out or move it right, dammit? You're teasing the literal shit out of me and I can't tell whether I'm starting to like it or have to fart!''

He laughed and said, ''Relax and try. You'll find you can't till I pull the cork.''

She snapped, ''Bastard!'' and he could tell from her rippling internal contractions she was trying to blow him out the back door. It felt neat.

She said, ''Hmm, that does make it more comfortable, albeit confusing as the devil. Is it really possible to climax this way, Deek?''

He reached down around her waist to start toying with her from the front as he humped her from the back, saying, ''With a little help from your friends. I may as well be a good sport about this, since you're turning out to be such a gracious hostess, red.''

She hissed in delight and started moving her hips as he began to strum her banjo with his fingers while he thrust in and out from behind. He'd have come long ago had it not been for earlier orgasms. For, now that she was getting into it, old Rubia really was a great lay, if that was what you wanted to call this.

She raised her bare torso from the desk like a sea lion standing on its flippers and threw her head back to wave her red hair all over the place as she moaned, ''Oh, my God! I'm coming with it up my ass and I think I just discovered America!''

He discharged his weapon, too, as she suddenly fell flat and limp with head and shoulders hanging over the far edge of the desk as she crooned, ''Oh, thank you for opening the gates to hidden gardens of delight, Deek. I've always wondered why some women said they liked it that way. I see, now—it's like learning to swim. You have to stay in the water until it seems more comfortable, no?''

He withdrew, looking for something to wipe off on. This

just wasn't his night. He'd started out to punish a teasing bitch, and damned if she hadn't enjoyed it as much or more than he had!

In the morning after breakfast, Sergeant Muldoon escorted Captain Gringo and a work detail to the trading post and armory to get them geared up. When asked, Muldoon said the officers were still sleeping. Lieutenant MacLean's orders were that he wanted them to be clear of the post before he got up. It figured. The brass was covering its tracks in case the London *Times* ever wondered just who'd done what, with what, to whom. The polite but coldly correct Muldoon was only an enlisted peasant who didn't have to recall all the details as he carried out his orders without questioning them. If neither the major nor MacLean even waved bye-bye as they marched out, they could say they were hazy on future details, too.

Muldoon was neither friendly nor unfriendly as he vouched for Captain Gringo at the trading post. He was even a good sport about letting the guerrillas stock up on more tobacco and medicinal rum, in case they ran into snakes. Captain Gringo loaded his men with field rations and camping gear and asked about ammo.

Muldoon led him along a veranda under an overhead tin awning. They went in. The stone-walled interior was piled high with cases and gun racks. Muldoon said he could have anything he could carry out alone, but that the officers had limited the giveaway to what one strong man could pack. Captain Gringo said that sounded fair and strolled over to the nearest pile of cases. He started to say he couldn't use British army ammo. Then he noticed the lettering stenciled on the ammo boxes and asked, "When did you guys switch to .30-30, sarge?"

Muldoon smiled thinly and replied, "Since we found out Remington ammo was cheaper and easier to find in these parts than Armstrong. We're not regular army, thank God, and when we need bullets to civilize the dons, we need it in massive doses. Our weapons are chambered for Yank ammo. Half the people we take guns away from can say the same. Are you really worried about British military regs, Walker?"

"Not now, but I was. I noticed your Lieutenant MacLean was a pretty slick pro. Using easy ammo makes sense. So, okay, I think I can carry at least a couple of cases of this .30-30."

He started to reach. Muldoon said, "You don't want that. Over here. We'd better check and make sure this fresh .30-30 is still bright and brassy."

He helpfully pried open the top of a case as Captain Gringo asked, "What was wrong with that other ammo?"

Muldoon said, "The tropics. Some ass shipped that lot lightly greased. A little green on the brass might not hurt, but you wouldn't want to load your Maxim with stuff that could have corroded primers!"

The tall American said, "You are so right. Thanks," as he examined the heavily greased cartridges in the suggested case. The rounds were loose, but he had his ammo belt and the men had clips for their liberated Krags.

He shut the case and said, "Two of these should do it. We can't carry much more. What other kinds of goodies do you have here, sarge?"

Muldoon said, "I could let you have a dozen Mills bombs."

"Are those those new grenades you don't have to light the fuses for?"

"They are. Just got some in. Pull the ring and throw 'em from cover. Good cover. When they go off they blow cast-iron fragments in every damn direction. Don't fancy Mills bombs myself. Civilize the blighters with butt stock and bayonet, I always say."

Captain Gringo thought and said, "I think I'll go along with you on the fancy new grenades. Some of my guys are as likely to throw the ring and hold the Mills bomb in their teeth. Haven't time to train 'em, and the cast-iron parts add up to extra weight. Got any dynamite?"

"Of course. How much do you think you can carry? It's sixty percent Nobel. The real thing. Couple of sticks planted under a wall ought to blow it halfway to the flaming moon."

Captain Gringo agreed. So Muldoon rummaged for the dynamite, fuse coils, and blasting caps as the soldier of fortune balanced one case of .30-30.

Muldoon brought the blasting gear, placed it atop the small-arms ammo, and said, "That ought to do you. Sure you can carry all that?"

Captain Gringo could. He'd have felt better about it in his legs if he hadn't fooled around with two women the night before. He staggered out of the armory with his load. As they crossed the parade, Muldoon said, "I'm not supposed to do this, but what the hell, anyone can see you took no more than you could carry."

He relieved Captain Gringo of the blasting gear. The American said, "Thanks. About the women we're leaving behind: the redhead is the easiest to get into, and about the most fun once you do."

"I'll keep that in mind, if my Mosquito squaw gets out of line. Our orders are to leave your dependents alone as long as they behave."

"That's good to hear. Don't tell my men. Soldiers fight better when they worry about the girl they left behind them."

Muldoon smiled thinly and said, "You can call them soldiers if you like, I suppose. They look like a mob of dagos to me."

"It's a good thing you don't have to lead them into combat, then."

"What combat? Mopping up a rat's nest of niggers and

half-breeds? This whole ruddy intrigue is a lot of rubbish, if you'd like my professional opinion. Give me and my buckos the go-ahead and we'd level the beggars in an hour or less.''

"Have you ever *seen* one of these cultists you're not so worried about, Muldoon?''

"Hell, Yank, what would there be to see in this soggy perishing dago country? Their bloody *military* couldn't hold off a raiding party of the Pathans we used to brush with on the old Northwest Frontier. Their idea of fighting down here is to shoot a priest, rape a child, and hold a perishing victory parade!''

Captain Gringo didn't answer. He didn't know why *he* should feel so annoyed. There was some truth in the burly Brit's comments on the ways of the Latin warlord. But he'd soldiered enough down here to know that there were brave men and women everywhere, and for guys sent to keep the peace in these parts, this outfit's attitude toward the natives needed some improvement.

Captain Gringo had met men like Muldoon before, when he'd served along the Mexican border. Anglo Saxons who'd run to size and read about the Alamo could too easily assume that they had an edge on any Hispanic they met. Quite often they got away with it. The average peon, like the average poor farmer of any culture, did tend to edge nervously away when a big blond guy a head taller than him made loud noises at him in a strange lingo. But it still wasn't a good idea.

He remembered that guy in Nuevo Laredo, that night. The guy had been big and built like a wrestler, with a foghorn voice that should have scared even *himself*. Captain Gringo hadn't gotten into it. He'd always assumed that if God wasn't protecting drunken fools, He wasn't interested in them.

The big Anglo bully had swaggered in loaded for bear and meanmouthing Mexico from the Baja to Quintana Roo. Most of the Mexicans in the cantina had done just what Yanks in a saloon would have done. They'd moved as far away from the obvious trouble as possible.

All but one. A vaquero drinking pulque at the bar and standing maybe five-foot-four in his high heels had listened with courteous attention until the Anglo got around to commenting on his sissy sombrero. Then, without putting down his drink, the vaquero had simply hauled out a big dragoon .45, blown the loud-mouth's head half off with point-blank fire, and strolled off through his own gunsmoke, muttering about the way Neuvo Laredo had once been such a nice quiet town.

But Muldoon's overconfidence was Muldoon's problem. They weren't sending the big sergeant to do anything to anybody. They were sending him. So Captain Gringo thanked him graciously when they had the ammo and explosives over in their part of the compound, near the other piled supplies.

Muldoon said they were all set and started to turn away. Captain Gringo said, "Hold it. One last favor. We don't have a map."

Muldoon said, "I'm going to get your maps from the Mosquito village to the south. We're sending four guides with you, as the lieutenant ordered."

"Swell. But shit, Muldoon, I don't even know where this place *is*! That old mission has to be a full day's march into even greater confusion!"

The noncom shrugged and said, "You can't have the map in the major's office. He needs it. The Indians can get you there and back. I'll fetch them now. When they show up, be ready to move out."

Muldoon marched off as if on parade. Gaston drifted over to say, "Eh bien, I am as anxious to see the last of these triple-crossers as they are to send us on our triple-crossed way. Do not concern your pretty little head about maps, Dick. I know where we are now."

"Is it a secret, you old goat?"

"Mais non. A few moments ago I took a stroll upon the parapet. I was chased down, for reasons of state, no doubt. But I got a look at the surrounding country. There is a boat landing to the east, on an oxbow of the Rio Negro. One of the Rio Negros, at any rate."

"*One* of the Rio Negros, Gaston? How many Rio Negros do they have in one damned country?"

Gaston shrugged and replied, "Oh, dozens. Any modest jungle stream running black as ink with tannin tends to be called the Rio Negro, locally. The only one along *this* stretch of the Mosquito Coast is between Monkey Point and the Rio San Juan del Norte. So I know where we are, hein?"

Captain Gringo frowned as he pictured his own version of the Nicaraguan map and said, "Hey, that won't work. That puts us well *north* of Greytown and even farther from the border than I thought. MacLean told us we'd overshot Greytown."

"Oui, he lied. For the same reason they do not seem to have an official map for us, no doubt. It occurs to me that what we have here is a très crude land grab, even by Queen Victoria's standards. I would never be rude enough to suggest the Brits have built a military outpost miles outside the boundaries of the treaty Washington thinks it signed. But we are still on the Rio Negro, deep in territory even an Englishman must sense is Nicaraguan."

Captain Gringo thought, nodded, and said, "Okay, so Whitehall's getting piggy again, like it did in Venezuela that time we gave the U.S. Marines a hand. What do you think the score is on that mission off to the west?"

"Merde alors, what is there to think, Dick? The drinkers of lime juice are already trespassing on Nicaraguan soil. They don't want anyone to notice until they are well established and no doubt swing a deal with the side they are backing in the civil war. I'm betting on that side, too, no matter which it is. Please do not be insulted when I say that your State

Department has a lot to learn from the ever so stuffy gentlemen in London.''

"Yeah, yeah, I heard about the Opium War, and all *we* ever got out of China was a mess of laundrymen. Are you saying go or no-go? That cult convent figures to be farther from the border than they told us, too. So what's the catch?''

"For us? Probably bullets to catch with our teeth. For the Brits, no doubt more Indians they'll have to reluctantly take under the wing of the British Lion, if one may mix his metaphors almost as convincingly as the British Lion does. The deal for us is a lot of trouble for très modest rewards. How much can it cost them to scribble a few words on paper and refrain from shooting our adorable derrieres off?''

Captain Gringo signaled Perrito to join them and said, "That's reward enough, when you consider the alternatives. Perrito, divide up all this shit so every man carries an even part of it. I'll pack my machine gun, and Lieutenant Verrier here will lug the machine-gun ammo and high explosives. Get moving. We'll be leaving any minute.''

Perrito jogged back to the others, shouting orders. Gaston observed, "Careful, Dick. You know what happens when you let a private begin to feel like a general.''

Captain Gringo said, "Perrito's okay. He's almost as old a survivor as you. Smart guys don't pull dumb stunts. He knows he's little, a stranger to most of the guys, and that the minute he got rid of us he'd have to start watching his own back. That's why I picked him to play top kick. Old Julio can get the others to go along with him. But old Julio just wants to go home a lot.''

"Eh bien, why not leave him here with the other useless baggage?''

"No man who can carry food and ammo is useless. Heads up, here comes Muldoon with some shills for a cigar store.''

The sergeant had returned with four Mosquito Indians. All wore floppy straw hats and carried machetes almost as big as they were. Their costumes resembled those of Florida Seminoles. That seemed reasonable. Two were men and two were female. That didn't seem reasonable and was hardly fair. His guys didn't get to take their adelitas along.

Muldoon introduced the two squat, sullen-looking men as Pat and Mike. He had no jokes to offer about the two squaws. The one the Brits had Christened Pat said, "Hail Mary, full of gracias. Do not beat me, I am a Cristiano!"

Mike didn't say anything. He just glared.

The two women looked out from under their hat brims with about as much enthusiasm. It was hard to see enough of either their faces or figures to tell if they were pretty or ugly, thin or fat. All that was for sure was that all four of them were either standing in holes in the ground or Mosquito Indians didn't grow much.

Gaston asked Muldoon if their guides ever acted as bearers. Muldoon said, "I wouldn't try to get them to carry any loads for you. You'd likely never see either them or the load again. I don't think they'll run off on you if you keep them well fed and only kick them when they know they deserve it."

"What if they desert us in the jungle for no sensible reason?"

"Oh, you'll be lost then, won't you?"

Muldoon marched away, not looking back. The two soldiers of fortune exchanged glances. Captain Gringo said, "Right. Let's get the show on the road."

He started walking over to the others to gather the men and his gear for the march. The Indians followed, silently as cats and with the same wary tenseness of strange cats in a strange house.

He ignored them and told Gaston, "I hope we can say adiós to the girls without a lot of blubbering. We'd better not let them walk out a ways with us, even if these Brits would go for it."

Gaston said, "Eh bien. I think I've said my good-bye

properly to Rubia in any case. As a matter of fact, you would have been proud of me, Dick, if I'd invited you to watch.''

"I was busy saying adiós to Lolita. What did I miss?"

"An astounding performance, even for me. I seem to have satisfied the redhead at last!"

"Oh?"

"Oui, the last time I laid her she begged me to stop. She said she'd been so thoroughly screwed she would not be able to walk for days. I knew all she needed was one good man to give it to her the right way!"

Pat and Mike led them into the fresh-water swamps to the west, which was to be expected. But they found themselves walking dry-shod, which hadn't been. The Indians knew their way around on the Mosquito Coast, which was no doubt why they were called the Mosquito Indians. The belt of cypress swamp inland from the cuesta, like most swamps, was dotted and dashed with bridges of floating mat or even solid muck to the bottom. The apparently solid ground quivered like jelly under them where the Indians led them across in a series of hairpin zigzags, but not even Captain Gringo broke through, machine gun and all. As they circled a lake of water as dark as India ink, Gaston observed, "Regard the source of the local Rio Negro. The outlet must be well to the south, and then it oxbows around closer to the post we just left. I am fond of black water. It's the one place those très fatigué mosquitoes don't breed. Our little friends of course know how to avoid their namesakes, bless their pagan hearts.''

Pat had keen ears. He glared back over his shoulder and snapped, "I am no pagan! Hail Mary full of gracias!" So Gaston shut up for a while. The explosives and spare ammo were already getting heavy and the so-called ground was tiring to walk on as it sagged under his weight.

Despite the detours, they made good time getting to the far side of the black-water swamp. That's when they found out why the Indians carried lots of machetes. The higher but still soggy soil on the far side was rich in nutrients for jungle soil, so both swamp and dry-land growth competed for root space and grabbed for the skylight cheek-to-jowl in a solid hedge of spinach. Pat waded into it like he knew where he was going, swinging his machete like a mechanical man.

Even mechanical men had limitations. So Mike and even the two women took turns in the lead without breaking the monotonous rhythm of wet machete slashes. Captain Gringo made a mental note to warn his guerrillas not to mess with either of those short brown chunky dames. A lady who could fell a substantial sapling with one backhanded machete blow was not a lady to mess with. He could see why their Indian wards made the constabulary a little nervous. Male or female, they were tough little bastards.

After what seemed a million miles of thick tangle they broke through the heavy growth into the cathedral gloom of classic tropical rain forest. The massive trees on either side rose forever on butressed roots to vanish high above in a stained-glass roof of beer-bottle green. The forest floor, where no tree chose to grow, was covered with what looked like soggy black roofing felt and mushrooms. Pat took the lead again and pressed on. If he was following a trail, Captain Gringo couldn't see it. But apparently Pat knew the way, so what the hell.

The Indians didn't just know the way. They seemed to be trying to get there the day before yesterday. Despite their short legs, they set a killing pace. Captain Gringo knew he and Gaston could keep up, even packing heavy loads. But the men staggering and cursing behind them were not legged-up infantry and each man was loaded with heavy gear. So when they topped a modest rise and he saw the ground cover was dry as an old black blotter, he called a trail break.

The Indians looked confused and perhaps a bit disdainful as the peones dropped their packs and rifles with relieved sighs and either went off to take a leak behind a tree or simply flopped beside their loads.

Captain Gringo placed the Maxim atop Gaston's rope-slung load and deliberately stayed on his feet to set an example and make sure everyone was okay before he rested his own weary butt. He took out some smokes. He called the guides over and said, "We'll rest here a minute. Here, have some tobacco."

Pat and Mike exchanged thoughtful glances. Pat hesitated and said, "Hail Mary full of gracias. You wish to give us *tobacco*, señor?"

"No, I'm holding it out in hopes some parrot will swoop down and take it out of my hand. What's the matter, Pat, don't you guys smoke?"

"We do, but seldom with your kind and never for free. El señor is most simpatico. Perhaps we shall take one of those beautiful cigars and share it. With your permission."

"Take all four, unless the girls don't smoke. I picked up plenty of smokes at the trading post back there. Why are you guys so nervous, Pat? Am I that frightening?"

Pat burbled something to the others in his low liquid tongue. They blew bubbles back at him, and one of the women even laughed. He took off his sombrero with a flourish and accepted the cigars, saying, "El señor is not frightening, but Hail Mary full of gracias, he is unusual for an Englishman!"

As he doled out the smokes, Captain Gringo explained, "I'm not an Englishman. I think I know what you mean, but as long as you're with us you share the smokes and rations equally, for as long as they hold out. How far do we have to go now, Pat?"

"It depends on how often we stop like this, señor. If we moved like Indians, we would be there by this time mañana. At the pace you set, it will take longer."

"So we'll take longer and get there full of fight. You'd better light up now. When I finish my own smoke, we'll be moving on."

The four Indians moved off to hunker down, heads together, and burble about crazy white men as they lit the unexpected gift cigars. Captain Gringo sat down by Gaston and the gear. Gaston said, "Be careful you don't spoil them, Dick. Both the local Creoles and their new English masters have accustomed them to a firmer hand on the reins."

Captain Gringo lit his own smoke before he snorted in disgust and said, "I noticed. They used to tell me I had to keep my black cavalry troops in the old tenth in their place. I treated 'em like human beings anyway. When they soldiered under me against the Apache, they obeyed my orders just like white troops would have. Matter of fact, they saved my ass a couple of times in battle."

"So I see, since your adorable ass is still with us. But you are speaking of your American colored people, not primitive savages. Until most recently our little friends ran naked through the forest, happily chopping strangers up as gifts of love to their primitive gods. Some suspect they still do so, when they get the chance."

"Okay, if they cut my head off for giving them some cigars I'll never speak to you again. I see the ground keeps rising. Aren't there some fair-sized hills between the east coast and the big inland lakes, Gaston?"

"Oui; in places one would call them mountains rather than hills of any size. The British plot grows thicker. This mysterious mission no doubt is a source of more than one annoyance to the expansionists back there. I have mixed emotions about Jesuits, ever since my parents tried to cure me of a pratique approach to private property in my youth by sending me for a time to a Jesuit school for wayward boys. But before I ran away I learned the so-called Soldiers of Christ were très pratique too. If the Jesuit order built the original mission amid all this grossly overgrown salad, one can bet on it that the mission dominates some well traveled Indian trail. No doubt the only one through some vast section of the jungle as well."

Captain Gringo nodded thoughtfull and replied, "I didn't think Queen Vickie was as interested in the mental health of the local primitives as she is in setting up a good defense line on her new borders. But ours is not to reason why and all that rot."

Gaston regarded the tip of his own cigar reflectively as he said, "I fail to share your British patriotism, my idealistic adventurer. Has it occurred to you we are already clear of the coastal swamps, and still outside the war zone to the west around the lakes?"

"Sure. The mission, convent, voodoo temple, or whatever probably holds a pass in country too rugged and empty to attract either army."

"Eh bien. If we were to move on just to easier high ground, and swing south, alone, an easy scamper would see us to Costa Rica and that nice hotel bar in San José, non?"

"There you go again. Our followers are depending on us to get them back to their adelitas and safe conduct to Greytown, dammit!"

"Merde alors, there *you* go again! We intended to leave Rubia and your Lolita behind in Greytown in any case, no? Eh bien, they shan't cry any harder if we simply never bother coming back. If we leave these no-doubt resourceful peones to work things out for themselves, they can find their way back to the coast just by splashing downhill with or without the Indians. What can those Brits do to them after they stagger in empty-handed, eat them? Neither our guerrillas nor the adelitas are wanted by anyone on serious charges. Whores and dishwashers are always in demand in any colony."

"Okay, but what if they send our people back to Nicaragua?"

"Mon Dieu, all of them *are* Nicaraguans, Dick! Use your

adorable blond head. The odds are the Brits won't put themselves to the trouble to deport perfectly serviceable peasants. Even if they do, they'll no doubt do so by contacting some reasonably civilized Nicaraguan authorities. Those wild troops who started all this nonsense by seizing that fishing village up the coast won't be the ones the Brits will turn our people over to. By now those uniformed bandits have doubtless moved on anyway. We agreed their rather severe security measures were probably connected with smuggled arms from the sea. Why should they hang on to the tiresome little place once they *have* their smuggled supplies, hein?"

"Hmm, that's a point I hadn't considered. If we backtracked and made sure those maniacs had moved on, our peones would be even happier in their old village than sweeping out waterfront saloons in Greytown, right?"

Gaston slapped his own forehead and muttered, "Me and my big mouth!"

Then he said, "Eh bien. That may in the end be the best place for our friends and followers. But I see no reason for you and me to go *anywhere* with them! I shall mention the possible safe return to Perrito or old Julio, très casually, as we wander about until nightfall. With luck they should desert us before we have to desert them. Once free of excess asses to worry about, you and me and that Maxim can go anywhere we wish, non?"

Captain Gringo shook his head and said, "I told them I'd get 'em back to their girl friends once we completed the mission. Wait, there's more. MacLean knows who we are, and a soldier of fortune with a rep for ducking out on a mission can have a tough time getting hired in the future."

"Merde alors, it is our *future* I am discussing, Dick! What contract would we be breaking? MacLean offered us no money. We simply made a verbal agreement that I doubt very much he wants to ever read about in the newspapers."

"True. But a deal is a deal and word always gets around.

Let's move it out. Rest too long on this leaf mold and you're
sure to wind up with stiff joints."

He rose to his feet and called out that they were pushing
on. As the others got up and hoisted their loads, one of the
Indian women came over to Captain Gringo. She was still
smoking the cigar he'd given her. In a small shy voice she
said in Spanish, "There is nothing ahead for me to chop
down. Is it permitted for me to carry for you, señor?"

He started to say no. Then he reconsidered and said, "You
may carry the machine gun, if you don't drop it. I can get at
my pistol easier if I'm free to move. How are you called,
señorita?"

She shook her head and said, "Por favor, I am not a
señorita, I am only an Indian. You would not be able to
pronounce my tribal name. The white missionaries named me
Barbara. I do not mind if you call me that."

He laughed and said, "Okay, Babs. Let me put this Maxim
on your shoulder and we'll see if it's too heavy for you."

The little squaw stuck her machete in the ground, took the
bulky machine gun and raised it in both hands, then balanced
it on the crown of her sombrero, saying, "It is not too
heavy." Then she dropped one hand to arm herself with the
machete again and turned gracefully away to walk off with the
Maxim balanced on her head like a tray of fruit.

Captain Gringo took a case of ammo and told Gaston to
worry about the explosives. Gaston said, "Eh, bien, the
dynamite is lighter. I think she likes you, Dick. Face was not
bad, and look at that nice manner she has in moving her
derriere!"

Captain Gringo laughed, told him he was a dirty old man,
and walked on behind Barbara. She did move her little butt
nicely under that striped pleated skirt. What he'd seen of her
face under the broad straw brim of that massive hat hadn't
been too awful or he'd have noticed. But save for a general

impression of a small brown okay face and a pair of big deerlike eyes, she hadn't left much of a portrait in his mind.

He stopped watching her ass as they moved to yet higher ground. He couldn't really tell what she was built like, and anyway, messing with Indian girls could make life needlessly complicated. She had to be the adelita of either Pat or Mike, since they were evenly matched in gender. The other Indian squaw had taken a cigar, but hadn't even said thank you, and for all he could see from here she could be the better-looking of the pair.

Great minds ran in the same channels. Gaston said, in his version of English, "If we took the women with us, our trek south would no doubt be even more enjoyable, non?"

"Jesus, Gaston, don't you ever think of anything else? First you talk about deserting our own guys and now you're suggesting we knock off a pair of so-far-friendly Indians!"

"Mais non, the thought never crossed my mind. Naturally we would give them something for the women. Indian women are trade goods, not objects of tender romance. The Brits won't let the tribe have any guns and ammo. If Pat and Mike could return to their tribe with a couple of rifles and some ammo, they would be able to retire as respected chieftains, non?"

"Knock it off, you old rogue. If you're going to chicken out on me, do it and get it over with. You know I'm going to do or die, and this conversation is getting tedious as hell!"

"So is this hike. But lead on, MacDuff. I keep telling myself to desert you before you finally manage to get us both killed, but perhaps you are the son I never had, unless, of course, I am fruit for you. Did anyone ever tell you what a nice derriere you had, Dick?"

"Yeah, you. We'll be done with this mission and back in Costa Rica long before either of us is tempted to bend over for the soap. That's if you just keep picking 'em up and laying 'em down. The ground's getting firmer. You're probably right about a pass. Old Pat's leading us in a westbound beeline now, and it's all uphill.''

Gaston didn't answer. The long gentle grade was rough on a guy's breath, packing a load and trying to keep up with a bandy-legged walking machine like their Indian guide.

They moved on and on. Sometimes the Indians led them downhill for a change, and in places they had to wade in ankle-deep muck as black as ink and smelling like puked bananas. But always on the far side of the muck-filled draws the ground rose a little higher than before. Captain Gringo called trail breaks from time to time, of course, and when it got really hot, even in the shade, he announced la siesta and rations all around.

The Indian women built a small smokeless fire when their male companions told them to. All four of them seemed confused but hardly upset when the strange blanco they'd been ordered to guide fed them beans, bully beef, and coffee, just like everyone else. The after-dinner cigars passed out to everyone even made the other and still-sullen squaw say something that sounded nice in her soap-bubble lingo.

As they rested and smoked, Captain Gringo consulted Pat about possible campsites for later that night, saying, ''We'll move by moonlight until the moon goes down. Then we'd better hole up. Where do you suggest?''

''Hail Mary full of gracias, el señor wishes to hear *my* opinion?''

''Of course. You know this country and we don't, Patricio.''

''Es verdad, but when we lead those soldados in the funny hats, they tell *us* where we should make camp. I have never understood why Englishmen wish for to camp near mosquito ponds, but when you ask them, they call you names.''

''It's a custom of theirs I don't understand either. Can you and Miguel show us a good campsite where we'll be safe from prowling scouts of those cultists as well as insects?''

''Of course. We are still too far from the Sisters of Santaria for to worry about them. Forgive me, I mean no disrespect, but at the pace you are setting, we shall not reach the old mission before nightfall mañana.''

"Bueno. That's a good time to move in on old missions. I'll leave tonight's campsite to you and your friends. Let's talk about our final goal. Have either you or Miguel been there?''

Pat made the sign of the cross and said, ''Hail Mary full of gracias, I am no follower of Santaria! They are devil worshippers, señor!''

"So I hear. Lieutenant MacLean said one of his Indian scouts had located the headquarters of the cult. I take it he wasn't talking about any of you?''

"Es verdad. We know the general area of those terrible people. We have to, lest we fall into their hands and spill our blood on the altar of their pagan gods. But none of us have ever been within sight of the mission walls. It is surrounded by cultivated corn milpas. The cultists grow beans and plantanas as well. When one follows this trail to where the jungle ends, one turns back, if he or she is Cristiano!''

"We've been following a trail? Never mind, I guess we must have been if you're not as lost as I am. Okay, I get the picture, sort of. The old Spanish mission's surrounded by open farmland. How much open space do we have to cross to hit the mission itself, Patricio?''

"Por favor, I do not know, señor. A kilometer, maybe five. Maybe more. Quien sabe? None of us have ever left the treeline for to be killed by those terrible people!''

Captain Gringo muttered, ''Oh boy, talk about a pig in a poke!''

Gaston had been listening with interest. He asked the guide, ''If none of you Mosquitoes are in any contact with those Santaria cultists, I find it très curious that they seem to be stirring up trouble among your tribesmen, Patricio.''

Pat looked blank and said, ''Not among my particular

band, señor. Perhaps other Mosquitoes further from the constabulary post have forgotten they are good Cristianos. Hail Mary full of gracias, my people fear the Sisters of Santaria even more than they fear our new Queen Victoria. She is said to be very stern, but at least she, too, is Cristiano, and so far the British have never killed anyone unless they deserved it.''

Captain Gringo frowned and asked, ''How does an Indian qualify for a British hanging these days, Patricio?''

The guide said, ''They do not hang us when we are bad, señor. They shoot us. Mostly for stealing. My people are poor. Sometimes they shoot people who are not willing workers.''

Captain Gringo growled, ''Jesus, that's chattel slavery, Gaston!''

Gaston shrugged and said, ''I believe they call it coolie labor in most of the pink parts of the map, Dick. It's not official, under current British law. But men who wander about with a swagger stick in one hand and a gin and tonic in the other can become très moody in a hot climate. Let us not concern ourselves with British colonial policy. Let us worry about the even stranger people to the west, or, even better, let us wonder if those adorable girls we left in San José are still waiting for us as they promised they would forever when we kissed them bye-bye a few months ago.''

Captain Gringo told him to shut up and finished his cigar deep in thought. There was no sense trying to get more details out of their poor ignorant guides, and MacLean, the bastard, was probably enjoying his gin and tonic miles to the east right now.

A million years later it felt a little cooler down among the buttress roots, so Captain Gringo ordered a resumed march. He was sorry he had as soon as he'd walked a few more miles. It wasn't all that hot in the afternoon jungle shade, but the humidity was at least ninety-nine and it was all uphill now. Little Barbara, up ahead, had to be sweating like a pig inside her cotton, packing that Maxim. But she wasn't bitching and he was too sticky to feel gallant.

The slope leveled off as it stayed damp but started to get darker. He hauled out the cheap pocketwatch he'd picked up at the trading post and saw it was the sun going down, not the canopy above getting thicker. They could still see okay. They'd move on until it got really dark, wait for the moon to rise, and see what they could see.

He decided to wait for another steep grade or total darkness, whichever came first, before calling a halt. He knew it would be a bitch to get his tired followers moving again once they stopped.

So the girl ahead was just a dark blur, and she must have been having trouble seeing, too, because she suddenly tripped over a fallen vine and fell on her face, machine gun and all.

He dropped his own load and moved forward to help her as she pulled herself into a ball of frightened flesh and pleaded, "Please don't beat me! The ghosts of the forest did it! I swear it wasn't *me*!"

He tried to help her up. She rolled away, sobbing. So he picked up the machine gun, ran his hands over the oiled steel to make sure it wasn't messed up with anything grittier than rotten leaves, and soothed, "Hey, nobody's going to hurt you, Barbara. Are you sure you didn't hurt yourself?"

"A little. I deserved it. The ghost tripped me and I tried to keep your beautiful gun from falling to the earth, but you know how ghosts are."

He hoisted the unharmed Maxim to one shoulder as Gaston and the others caught up. He waved them on and told the Indian girl, "You weren't tripped by a ghost. It was this vine here."

"Sí, the ghosts of the forest are tricky that way. Anyone can see it was a tree vine, on the forest floor where no tree vine is supposed to grow!"

"Yeah, it fell from the trees above. There's a lot of that going around. Are you really hurt?"

"No, just frightened, señor. I have done nothing to the ghosts of the forest. But now they have put me in position to be beaten by my master and it is enough to make one almost cry!"

He laughed and said, "Come on, let me help you up. I hardly ever beat ladies who pack machetes, and I'm not your master."

"You're not? Who are you if you are not my master? They told us back at the outpost we had to do everything you told us to do, no?"

"Okay, right now I'm telling you to take my hand and let me haul you up. These ghost stories are fun, Babs, but we've got a ways to go before we stop again, and the others are getting a good lead on us."

She gave him her hand timidly. He pulled her and her machete up. She kissed his wrist and said, "Oh, I see, you wish for to fuck me instead, no?"

"Whatever gave you that idea, honey?"

"It is the way with men and women who have been naughty. I should have known at once when you said you would not beat me that you had other punishment in mind. Men are never nice to women unless they desire for to fuck them, no?"

"Come on, Babs. I've got to get that ammo I dropped and catch up with the others. The missionaries who pounded Spanish into you sure went light on the morality jazz, I see, and they should have explained spiritual matters more thoroughly, too. Ghosts of the forest, sweet Santa Barranza!"

She followed him meekly as he strode on, carrying everything. He let her prattle on about ghosts, since it was sort of important to know how his Indians thought. Apparently they hadn't ever grasped the Baconian view of cause and effect. Like many tribal peoples, they refused to believe in accidental happenings. They were animists, under their thin veneer of Christianity, and so, since everything around them had a mind of its own, not even a vine could fall out of the canopy without some mind guiding it. They were smart enough to see that only living men and beasts ever made visible moves on their own. Ergo, spirits or ghosts had to be behind such mysterious happenings as tripping over something in the dark. It was no wonder the mosquitoes were easy to bully. The poor little guys and gals were scared skinny of the haunted world all around them!

They caught up easily enough. Gaston had taken it upon himself to call a break on a rise and issue rations. Captain Gringo didn't argue. He was tired, wet, and, now that it was really dark, cold. The trouble with the tropics was that it needed one of those new thermostats some electrical whiz had invented back home for people who didn't need them half as much.

The moon rose an hour or so later. It was no longer full and, of course, rose a little later every night as it lagged behind the sun. But when it got around to gracing them with its presence, the light was good enough to press on, so they did.

They made another ten or twelve miles before the slanting rays no longer made enough difference to matter. Captain Gringo called a final halt for night camp. They built no fires on the high dry ridge Pat had led them to. Everyone was so bushed they just unrolled their ground cloths and blankets and turned in. Captain Gringo thought about putting someone on picket duty. He knew he really should. But his men were tired to the point of mutiny, and who was going to creep up on them in total darkness, this far from anyone but Barbara's ghosts of the forest?

He set up the Maxim on the boxes near his own bedroll, checking the dubious canvas ammo belt by feel before locking the machine gun on safe with a round in the chamber. The canvas had started out coated with rot-resistant dubbing. Maybe it was still okay. Muldoon had been sort of vague about new belting, even though they had machine guns back at the outpost.

He undressed and balled his shirt and pants for a pillow, with the .38 under it. Then he got under the cotton flannel with a luxurious sigh. His head was still going a mile a minute, but the soft earth felt as good as a feather mattress under his weary bones. He had no idea why he had a hard-on and told it to lie down and behave.

It might have, had not a naked lady slid into the bedding with him. He couldn't see her, but there was no mistaking her costume as she snuggled her warm soft flesh against his. He whispered, "Barbara?" and she said, "Sí, I am ready, when you are."

He laughed and murmured, "I told you I'd forgiven you for dropping that gun. Of course, if this is your own idea... but what about your menfolk?"

"They were the ones who told us to sleep with you, querido."

"Oh? I see Gaston was right about trade goods."

He started to call out in the darkness to the Frenchman, but that would have been dumb. She'd just said they'd both been sent to service the master race, and if the other guys found out they'd been left out, it could mix them up needlessly. For a Frenchman, Gaston was taking silent advantage of manna from heaven. Gaston had probably come to the same conclusion about keeping a few secrets from the others.

Meanwhile, he had gone to bed alone with a hard-on, wasn't alone in bed anymore, so what the hell.

Barbara lay submissively beside him as he explored her body in Braille. She read nicely. He still wasn't sure what she looked like, but her small chunky body was a series of smooth firm curves, and when he kissed a nipple and ran his hand down her firm belly to home plate, he found she'd shaved or plucked her pubic hair.

As he cupped her childlike mons in his palm and explored deeper with one finger, she spread her solid brown thighs without comment. So he did what any gentleman would have done in his place. He rolled aboard.

She sucked in her breath as she felt him entering her. She was almost as tight as a little girl, too. Then she clamped on his questing shaft with internal muscle control few molested children could have managed. So they quickly became old friends, whatever she looked like in the light.

Like tribal women he'd made love to before, Barbara seemed to view sex as a natural appetite to be satisfied with no more bullshit than eating or drinking. It was a nice change. She responded with uncomplicated warmth and no coy resistance to his thrusts. She responded more, as she discovered he was willing to wait for her at the crossroads. He knew he could do anything to her. That made him feel obligated to be a considerate lover. He timed it so they climaxed together. She sighed and said, "Oh, I am so glad they told me to sleep with you, señor."

"Call me Dick, in bed. How come they ordered you girls to be so nice to us, Babs? Are Pat and Mike mariposas or are they just stupid?"

"I do not know. They are men, and women must never question the orders of men, no?"

"Boy, it's a good thing I'm not the Marquis de Sade!"

"Who is he, Deek?"

"Never mind. I hope you never meet a guy like that, kitten. You wouldn't stand a chance."

She yawned and asked, "Could we either do it some more or go to sleep, por favor?"

He laughed and started moving in her again until she decided she wasn't sleepy after all. She was game for any position and probably would have let him abuse her. But he didn't. He knew if he hurt her, some dumb ghost would get the credit, and right now he wanted her all to himself.

They found out how they'd been suckered, by the cold gray light of dawn. Obviously neither of the Indian girls had been let in on the plan or they'd have been long gone with Pat and Mike. Their male guides had taken some food but hadn't stolen anything important. The girls said the boys had probably been frightened. They were frightened of the witches up ahead, too, of course, but they were only women, so what could they do?

Gaston's bed partner had turned out to be Maria. Dressed again but without their sombreros they were both nice-looking— an obvious complication unless they wanted to take on some gang-banging. Over breakfast Captain Gringo questioned them about the route ahead. Neither had much knowledge of the country this far west. They said they'd come along with Pat and Mike because Pat and Mike had asked them to.

Gaston said, "Eh bien, without guides, it is useless to push on, non?"

Captain Gringo told him to shut up and asked Barbara if she and Maria could get back to their village on their own, given the machetes and some rations.

Barbara nodded, neither anxious nor apparently concerned either way as she said, "Of course. But we were told to be of service to you."

He smiled fondly at the vapidly pretty little innocent and said, "You sure helped me make it through the night, doll. But we don't want you to get hurt, and it's dumb to drag you along if you don't know the way."

The two Indian girls blew bubbles at each other, agreed they really didn't want to get killed if it would serve no useful purpose, and were last seen waving bye-bye with their machetes as Captain Gringo and the others pushed on. He was going to miss old Barbara, come bedtime. But she and Maria were two worries off his mind. He still had all the worries he needed to keep him from falling asleep on his feet as they plodded on.

The plodding improved after they found themselves going downhill for a change. They'd topped the long gentle rise of the north-south wrinkle in the rug of Nicaragua and the jungle floor sloped the other way at the same gentle grade.

After a while that got to be a pain in the ass.

Gaston protested, "Merde alors, walking on one's heels on banana peels is très fatigue, Dick. I know we could hardly be going below sea level as we slip and slide our jolly way, but one foresees more swamps ahead. Did anyone mention this mysterious mission being in a swamp?"

Captain Gringo said, "Nobody mentioned *where* the fucker is, exactly. Damn that MacLean for a tight-ass Scotchman with his ordnance maps. He might have known those Indian guides would punk out on us!"

"Mais oui. Has it occurred to you that might have been part of the plan, Dick?"

"Yeah, sending a small party out to do a big job does sound like a setup. But I can't figure any sensible motive. So, what the hell. If he hadn't expected us to come back alive, he'd have promised us the moon instead of just safe conduct to Greytown."

"True. But this très fatigué business still adds up to a feint in my military genius of a mind. A good tactition, like a good boxer, feints with a lackluster left before throwing the cocked right fist, non?"

"Hmm, could be. But we've taken the direct route. So if the Brits are planning to clobber that cult with a column of no-kidding constabulary troops, they don't figure to get there for a while. Another problem. We're pretty deep in Nicaraguan real estate right now. Uncle Sam ain't gonna like it if he ever hears about European invasions in bananaland. And there's no way even old Queen Vickie is ever going to sell this deep a penetration as anything else!''

They went on walking downhill and talking in circles until they saw a solid green wall ahead. Captain Gringo ordered his men to break out their own machetes and hack on through, explaining, ''We must be getting to another swamp or a break in the tall timber. Keep it down to a roar as you move through the spinach, muchachos. Those Indians said the target was surrounded by open farmland, and we've been on the trail awhile.''

That turned out to be the answer. Perrito, in the lead at the time, slashed halfway through a big squishy plantana, stopped when he saw through the gap of the leaning tree, and called Captain Gringo forward.

The tall American, with Gaston trying to read over his shoulder, stared out and down the open slope ahead. He whistled softly.

They were overlooking an open valley paved with a checked quilt of irrigation or drainage ditches and five- or six-acre crop milpas. Somebody was growing one hell of a mess of beans, corn, tobacco, and so forth. The cleared and cultivated area had to be a good ten square miles, strung out north and south in a shoebox, or coffin, shape. On the far side rose another jungle-covered ridge with a water gap cut through it. A sluggish stream oxbowed out across the valley floor, looped south, and vanished that way in the hazy distance. Tucked in a bow of the meandering unmapped river stood a massive complex of stone walls and red tile roofs. It was out of place for a robber baron's castle, so it had to be the mission of the Sisters of Santaria. It was set in a nice defensive position, with most of the approaches moated by the stream and nothing but lots of open ground facing the towers on either side of the main gate. Here and there across the valley they could make out the thatched roofs of scattered farm dwellings. Some of the milpas were surrounded by hedgerows or shelterbelts of shade trees. So taking a population census was tricky, but there had to be one hell of a population dedicated to the cult of Santaria in these parts.

Captain Gringo led everyone back to hold a council of war under the jungle canopy. He explained the setup to those who hadn't seen it and added, "Nobody seems to be working the fields this far upslope at the moment. But we can't break cover in broad daylight without being spotted from the towers of the old mission. On the other hand, if we wait until dark, we ought to be able to move in pretty close. We don't have to cross the river to work our way to the gates, and the ditches are narrow enough to jump over, so . . ."

"Forgive me, my captain," Perrito cut in, "the muchachos and me have been thinking."

Captain Gringo raised an eyebrow and asked, "Don't you mean talking behind my back, Perrito?"

"That too, my captain. I assure you, only with the greatest respect. You have saved us all more than once. We have no doubt you are one hell of a fighter and perhaps a good general. But, Jesus, Maria, y José . . ."

"Okay, out with it, Perrito. Are you suggesting you'd make a better leader than anyone else present and accounted for?"

"Madre de Dios, no! I saw what happened to the late Hachismo! I do not want your job. None of us want your job. It is just that, with all due respect, we think you are loco en la cabeza. You do not have the men and materiel for to attack stone fortifications! We love you. We respect you. But, forgive us, we do not wish for to die!"

There was a murmur of agreement from the assembly. Even Gaston said, "The man has a point, you know. Given a gun, three men, and a boy, I think I could hold that imposing pile of masonry against an army, which we are lacking. It would take field artillery to attack that position with any hope of taking it. And please do not prattle on about chinning

oneself quietly over the walls or creeping in through some
sewer drain as your ingenious Ethan Allan did at Ticonderoga.
Such weaknesses in a fortress are rare, even when the plans
were not drawn up by Jesuits to keep wild Indians at bay!''

Before Captain Gringo could reply, they all heard distant
drums. More than one, from the sound of it. Gaston cocked
his head thoughtfully to listen before he observed, ''Those
are not the old mission bells calling the faithful for quiet
prayer and meditation, Dick! Those are talking drums. African. I have heard them in Haiti and other parts where some
idiots made the mistake of enslaving African witch doctors. It
occurs to me they may be gossiping about us, hein?''

Captain Gringo frowned thoughtfully and said, ''I don't see
how we could have been spotted. Perrito, go forward and
keep a lookout down the slope.''

Perrito didn't move.

Tio Julio made the sign of the cross and protested, ''Forgive us, señor. You may be right. On the other hand, the
reason we saw nobody in those corn milpas just now could be
that they have been aware of us for some time and . . .''

Captain Gringo silenced the old man with a wave of his
hand and said, ''Okay, I get the picture. I hardly ever advance
on an unknown enemy if I'm not sure of the guys behind me.
But listen, muchachos, what about your adelitas back at the
British outpost? We can't go back to them empty-handed, you
know.''

Perrito nodded and said, ''We know. That is one of the
things we have been talking about among ourselves. We just
met the women, after all, and while some of us are quite fond
of our adelitas, a man can get another woman easier than he
can stand up with a bullet in him.''

Julio said, ''We have been thinking about those soldados
who swept into our old village. By now they should have left.
How much is there to steal in such a small fishing village?
Thanks to you and those British, we have guns, ammunition,

and supplies. We know the way back. So, with your permission . . .''

"Oh, shit, anyone who hasn't the balls to follow me can just take off!"

If he'd meant that to shame at least some of them into standing by him, it didn't work. Perrito nodded, said, "Vamanos, muchachos!" and took off. The others scooped up their packs and rifles and followed, calling out to Perrito not to run so fast.

Captain Gringo watched with disgust until he and Gaston were all alone with the machine gun, their other weapons, and supplies. Then he turned to Gaston and said, "Well, we seem to have separated the men from the boys. Any suggestions?"

Gaston said, "Oui. Let *us* be boys too. The border is *that* way!"

The tall American started to say something dumb about the safe-conduct papers to Greytown. Then he nodded and said, "You're right. Now that we only have our own asses to worry about, we can follow the treeline south out of sight of that whatever. We're inland far enough to walk dry-shod most of the way and we're far enough east to be out of the war zone, I hope. By the time MacLean figures out we're not coming back, we'll be enjoying decent cigars in San José, and they probably won't even lay the girls we left behind us, the stuffy bastards.''

He picked up the machine gun, said, "Fuck 'em all but six. We've got our own asses to worry about. Grab the explosives and ammo. I'll pack the grub. Let's go to Costa Rica, old buddy!"

"Now you are talking très reasonable, my adorable fuck-'em-all. But why pack the machine gun? We'll never be able to check into a decent hotel in San José with such luggage.''

"Right. Meanwhile, we still gotta get there, and I said I *hoped* we were clear of the war zone!"

Apparently they weren't. They moved south a few miles. Then Captain Gringo hacked out to open country with the Maxim on his shoulder and their one machete in his free hand, and they saw the jungle-covered ridge they were on was cut through ahead of them by a water gap and lots of ooze.

When they got to the sunny open slope beyond the brushy treeline, they were out of sight of the mission, although still in farmland probably cultivated by followers of the mysterious sisterhood. They got their bearings and Captain Gringo pointed across the valley with the machete to say, "We can cut straight across and ford the river where it's acting like a river. See how they've banked it above that oxbow?"

"Oui, very neat, I'm sure. But, sacre goddamn, Dick, it's broad daylight!"

"Big deal. There's nobody in sight. Those drums must have called all the local peones in for a powwow. I already thought about waiting till dark. There might not be time. They either know we're in the neighborhood or they don't. Either way, let's get the fuck *out* of it before they make up their minds what to do about us!"

As he broke cover and trudged boldly down the grassy slope with Gaston clucking behind him, he added, "If we were spotted up closer to the mission, they have us down as a larger party. That should make 'em dig in instead of boiling out at us. Hey, here's a neat path, leading right for that natural ford in the river ahead. I knew that was where you crossed if you wanted to. Do you know what river we're talking about, Gaston?"

Gaston shook his head and said, "Mais non. If I'd ever

been through here before I never would have let you lead me
back. I'd guess it was a tributary of some other river running
to the Caribbean. What difference does it make, since we
intend to cross the silly stream and keep going, hein?''

Captain Gringo agreed and followed the red dirty path
across the flat valley bottom to the crossing. There was a
milpa of standing corn on the far side, which seemed reason-
able. Some of the corn stalks were moving, which didn't.
There wasn't a hint of breeze in the muggy air around them.
It got worse when he looked around for cover and saw none.
They were surrounded by acres of freshly planted peppers.
The crop wasn't shin-deep yet!

Gaston had spotted the movement in the corn ahead and
dropped to one knee with his Krag sniffing the far side with
its muzzle. Captain Gringo threw the machete tip-down into
the red clay and swung the Maxim off his shoulder to train it
the same way, braced on his hip. That was when some son of
a bitch shot him in the head.

The tall American opened up with the machine gun,
traversing left to right at crotch level as corn stalks toppled,
unseen somebodies screamed, and blood ran down into his
eyes from the nasty scalp wound across the top of his dome.
The bullet had blown his hat off as it parted his hair lower
than he'd have done with a comb. But he knew he still had
his brains, so what the hell.

A straw hat flew up in the air as some spineshot invisible
enemy died amid the corn. Other stalks were moving as
others hastily moved back through the milpa they'd been
skulking in. Gaston was getting off rifle rounds as fast as he
could work the bolt of his Krag. A few wildly aimed shots
flew over them, but it took guts to stand and draw a bead
against automatic fire, and apparently the braver guys on the
far side of the stream had been out front and gone down in the
first unexpected burst of return fire—from a bloody mess that
was supposed to be dead. Captain Gringo made a grim

picture as he stood there glaring with slitted eyes and bared teeth through a mask of blood.

It was even starting to bother him. The scalp wound was bleeding like hell and the little pinwheeling stars before his eyes were trying to tell him he'd either have to put his head down and do something about the bleeding or just pass out on his feet.

He didn't stop firing. Neither did Gaston, until he'd emptied the rifle clip and reached for another. That was when Gaston saw what was coming up *behind* them!

He yelled, "Dick! We're surrounded!" and was still trying to reload his rifle when a huge Negro completed his wild charge across the peppers and knocked Gaston galley west with the flat of his machete.

Captain Gringo turned, groggy from loss of blood, and pulled the trigger of his Maxim as he faced the long ragged line of charging peones. Nothing happened. The belt had been used up. As the grinning gang of white, black, and in-between whatevers closed in on him and the downed Gaston, Captain Gringo dropped the Maxim, reached for his .38, and fell on his face in the peppers, muttering, "So long, world. It's just too much trouble standing up around here."

Somewhere someone was pounding the shit out of a big bass drum. So Captain Gringo opened his eyes. He didn't see anything. He was flat on his back in a pitch-dark room. He seemed to have wound up on some kind of a bunk. He called out, "Gaston?" and nobody answered. He gingerly raised a hand to his head. Someone had stitched his scalp back together. He was glad he hadn't been awake at the time. The surgical stitching was pretty neat. He felt they'd washed his hair as well as his face. They'd only shaved a strip where the bullet had plowed his head open. He checked the rest of him and discovered he was naked. He'd never missed his shoulder holster more. He threw off the thin cotton sheet and sat up, swinging his bare feet to a clammy stone floor. The effort sent a wave of nausea through him. He knew he could stand if he really had to. But he didn't have much fight left in him.

He growled, "The hell you say, tummy. We have to get you and our ass in motion. Those voodoo drums are right outside and you'll *really* feel sick if they're playing our song!"

A slit of light appeared as a door opened with someone holding a candle on the far side. As she came in, he saw it was a mighty spooky-looking lady in a dark blue nun's habit. Her face was even darker. The black nun in blue held the candlestick in one hand and a big china mug in the other. He wondered how she'd managed to unlock the door. She said, "I heard you cry out, Captain Gringo. Drink this. It will give you strength. You have lost much blood, but with the help of Santaria you should feel better soon."

He took the cup. But he didn't taste as he frowned up at her and said, "So you know who I am, huh?"

"We have been expecting you for some time. Why do you hesitate? Do you seriously suggest we would go to the trouble of treating your wound just so we could poison you?"

That made sense, and he was thirsty as hell. He took a cautious sip. It was hot chocolate laced with brandy. He took a couple of gulps and said, "I know a fat girl named Gordita who'd really go for this. I know some old Spanish legends, too. They say that when the Aztecs were fixing to carve a guy's heart out with a stone blade they fattened him up for a while first."

The black nun moved over to a shuttered window he of course hadn't known was there and threw it open. The drumbeats sounded louder. She said, "See for yourself if we are doing half the things our enemies say we do, Captain Gringo.''

He didn't move. He was bare ass naked under the sheet across his lap, and there she went with that Captain Gringo shit again. She sensed his hesitation and raised her candle to shed more light as she pointed at his clothing draped over a chair in the far corner. Everything had been laundered freshly. She said, ''I shall leave you to finish your cocoa and make yourself presentable for Mother Salome. I shall return in a few minutes.''

He said, ''Hold it, Sister, ah . . . ?''

''I am called Sister Lilith. What is it?''

''About my friend, and those guys I chopped up with a lot of your corn.''

She stared down soberly at him and said, ''M'sieur Gaston is recovering from his concussion in another cell, of course. As for the pobrecitos you cut down with your machine gun, there were twelve killed and as many wounded. We don't expect more than two of the wounded to survive. Alas, we have primitive medical facilities here at the Mission de Santaria.''

''Oh boy. I guess your mother superior is a little miffed at me, right?''

''Mother Salome shall discuss such matters with you, Captain Gringo. You will do well to dress quickly and not keep her waiting.''

She went out and shut the door behind her, leaving him the candle. He didn't hear her lock it. He gulped down the rest of the spiked chocolate, then muttered, ''The old cat-and-mouse shit, eh?'' as he tried again to rise. This time it worked. The deck swayed a little under him as he tottered over to his duds, but something in that drink besides the obvious had settled his stomach at least.

As he dressed he tried to make sense out of the black nun's weird words. He was no theologian, but some Sunday school had rubbed off. So he knew neither Salome nor Lilith were saints' names. They were bad girls, according to the Good Book.

He didn't find his .38 among his laundered belongings. He hadn't really expected to. He stomped on his boots and took advantage of the moment to peer out the window. If he'd been a Catholic he'd have made the sign of the cross. He was staring down into the now roofless nave of what had been the main chapel when some long dead Jesuit architect designed it. It was nighttime. He'd been out all day and then some. The moon was beaming down on a scene Dante might have written about. In the semidarkness, people of all shapes and sexes were slithering around on the bare dirt in their bare asses. Some few had peon costumes on and were just standing, watching, as the main celebrants of the mass of whatever formed a can of worms near the old stone altar. He couldn't tell if *everyone* in the pile-up was screwing or not, but some of them sure were. A naked Negro with his face painted white was crouching on the once Christian altar, pounding that damn noisy drum. He muttered, "So that's what a black Mass looks like, eh? I hope I'm not the main event!"

Sister Lilith knocked politely and, when he called, "Entrada!" came in to announce, "Mother Salome will see you now."

"Swell. I want to see her, too. Ah, do you sisters take part in those, ah, rites in you habits, Sister Lilith?"

The black nun frowned and replied, "Of course not. You must understand our congregation consists of rather primitive natives."

"I noticed," he replied, following her outside. She led him down a corridor and out through a cloistered garden. He knew he could easily overpower her and escape over the garden wall. But, dammit, they had poor old Gaston locked up somewhere. He had to go along with this cat-and-mouse shit until the chances looked brighter.

Sister Lilith opened a massive oak door and ushered him

inside. She didn't follow, but closed the door behind him as he found himself facing an imposing figure in a luxuriously appointed chamber. Mother Salome, if that was she, wore a blood-red nun's habit and stood at least six feet tall. Her white face hadn't been out in the sun much in recent memory. He couldn't see her figure in that quasi-nun's outfit. Her features were fine-boned but severe. She looked more like a very handsome young man in a ga-ga costume than a pretty woman. Her eyes were as green and as expressionless as those of a staring cat. She smiled thinly, indicated a seat on an iron-bound chest at the foot of a four-poster set in a corner, and, when he seated himself, parted the mosquito curtains of the four-poster to sit beside him on the mattress. Her voice was too high for a man's but mighty deep for a woman's as she said, "Your friend is still unconscious. We drugged him to keep him from thrashing about as he recovered from his concussion. I see you are feeling better, Captain Gringo?"

He stared beyond her at the morocco-bound volumes on the bookshelves lining her walls. He said, "You must read a lot. I'm awake again, I think, but I'm still confused as hell. Oops, forgot where I was."

She smiled slightly and said, "You need not concern yourself about profanity here. We are not a regular Catholic order."

"No kidding? Gee, I thought those were the Bells of Saint Mary banging away outside. Listen, ma'am, about those guys of yours we shot it out with. I know it may have seemed a little rude, but they shot at us first."

She shot him a puzzled frown and asked, "Guys of ours? Surely you do not think any of our followers would open fire on total strangers from a corn milpa?"

"Oh, right, the guy who clobbered Gaston was on *our* side."

"Of course. Naturally, when your friend looked as if he meant to shoot at them, too, they had to defend themselves."

He shook his head to clear it, found out that hurt like hell, and said, "I'm missing something here, Salome. Do you mind if I just call you Salome? I feel dumb calling a pretty lady 'my mother.'"

She smiled a little more warmly and said, "Among ourselves we do not have to be formal. In front of the pobrecitos, of course . . ."

"Gotcha. Let's get back to the pobrecitos in the cornfield. If they weren't with you, who were they with?"

She said, "We're not certain which so-called cause they pretend to. So many evil men waving the flag of either Granada or León are simply bandits these days."

He let out a sigh of relief and said, "Oh, now I'm starting to make sense! Gaston and I didn't tangle with your guys. We stumbled into a guerrilla coming up the valley the other way, right?"

"Yes, and we are most grateful. We have fought off more than one earlier raid by such scum, but we did not know they were approaching from the south. Our scouts reported armed men in the jungles to the northeast."

"Your scouts are good. Not to worry, Salome. Those were our guys, high-tailing it for home with free cigars from Queen Victoria. You, ah, did know Queen Victoria holds less unusual views on religion than you and your nuns, didn't you?"

She nodded soberly and said, "We were warned of your approach long before you were out of sight of that constabulary post. Some of my people wanted to ambush you in the jungle. I told them not to."

"Gee, that was swell of you, Salome. What did your Santaria spies tell you we were coming for, a friendly social call?"

She laughed lightly and said, "I knew the object of your

mission. I knew how the expedition would turn out. We are not as out of touch with the rest of the world as one might think. I knew those silly British were too, how you say, cheap, to mount a real expedition against us. I mean no disrespect, but starting out with a handful of mere peones with few military skills, you were, ah, licked before you started."

"I guess Gaston and me surprised you by not turning back with the others, eh?"

"On the contrary. I expected you two soldiers of fortune to push on. As I said, I keep abreast of events in the outside world. I have followed you career with considerable interest. Like me, you have a terrible reputation. But things are not always as they may seem. The authorities of more than one country would have it that you are a renegade and a killer. I know what you really are. That is why I was not afraid. I foresaw this meeting and knew it would be friendly."

He stared cautiously at her and said, "Hey, I'm willing to be pals if you are. You've got the drop on me."

She shot him a puzzled smile and asked, "Drop on you, Ricardo Walker? I assure you I am not carrying concealed weapons."

He said, "Neither am I. I used to have a machine gun and a pistol. But you know how things get kicked out of the way."

She said, "Your weapons are being cleaned and oiled. The canvas belt of your Maxim was badly frayed. I have ordered my sisters to stitch it more strongly and to copy it with spare canvas. My people salvaged many weapons and a great deal of ammunition that fits your machine gun from that corn milpa. Do you think two or three belts of .30-30 will be enough?"

"Enough to do what?" he replied cautiously.

She said, "To help us defend this mission, of course. As you just saw, we are not far from the war zone. So, roving bands of guerrillas have been giving us a very difficult time of late. Our prayers to Saint Mary, Mambo Jumbo, and other saints can only do so much. We must take practical steps as well. I knew when they told us you were coming to kill us with a Maxim machine gun that our prayers were answered!''

He started to point out how nutty that sounded. But maybe a lady who worshipped Christian and voodoo saints at the same time didn't think just the way he did.

He shrugged and said, ''You're welcome to the machine gun. It was getting heavy anyway. If you're saying Gaston and me aren't prisoners after all, we can't stick around to fight for Mumbo Jumbo, no offense.''

''But, Ricardo, you *must* stay here, just a little while. The civil war is coming to a head. Those English interlopers, too, must be held at bay until things settle down and your kindly President Cleveland has another discussion of the Monroe Doctrine with greedy Queen Victoria.''

He started to shake his head, but that hurt. So he said, ''Look, Salome. I don't know just what in hell you are, but Gaston and me are soldiers of fortune. We fight for *pay*. Okay, those cheap Brits didn't pay us anything but a few cans of bully beef, and we don't really need their dumb safe-conduct passes, so all bets are off and I'm starting to feel better about not crawling up your Ticonderoga with a machine gun. But, again no offense, I'm not about to join a voodoo cult!''

She rose imperiously and said, ''Santaria is not voodoo. You should not condemn something just because you do not understand it. You are still weak from loss of blood. A good night's sleep will clear your head. We shall talk about it some more in the morning.''

He rose too, asking, ''Are you saying you won't let us go, Salome?''

''Certainly not tonight, in your condition. Neither of you

are fit to walk five kilometers. You will stay in your cell tonight. In the morning we shall see what we shall see.''

She pulled a bell cord by the door. This time a nun with an Indian face and a mint-green habit opened it. Mother Salome told her to escort Captain Gringo back to his cell and make sure he was comfortable. Then she said good night, firmly, and shut the door after him with a not-too-happy slam.

He followed the Indian nun back to the same cell. He felt better about ''cell'' now that he saw they meant it in the convent usage. The short nun in pastel green took him there and shyly asked if there was anything she could do for him. He laughed and said, ''I forgot to borrow a book back there. Let's see, I'm not hungry, and I don't suppose a guy can get laid in a convent, so . . .''

Then he saw what the nun was doing and gasped, ''Hey, why are you taking off your clothes, sister?''

''Did you not say you wished for to lay me, señor?''

''I was kidding! Jesus, a warm meal and a good lay would kill me right now!''

She shrugged and smoothed her habit back in place. Not before he'd seen what she wore under it, which was nothing. She shaved *her* snatch, too. He sat down, laughing, and she left before he could ask her if the Sisters of Santaria all took such a casual attitude toward their vows. Then, as he undressed and went back to bed, he reflected that Mother Salome had said they weren't a regular Catholic order. So maybe they didn't take the same sort of vows, or any vows at all.

From the noise outside, the orgy was still going on. He snuffed the candle with a grin and muttered, ''Good thing Gaston's knocked out. By now he'd be down in the nave, worshipping hell out of Santaria, whoever she was and wherever he could get it in.''

He lay back and closed his eyes. He felt like he'd been

beaten all over with baseball bats, and every muscle in his body was aching to sleep at least a week.

Every muscle but one.

He snorted in disgust and said, "You stupid horny little bastard! You're tired, too, if only you had sense to do anything but pee or fornicate! Lie down like a good doggy, pecker. That dumb little nun wasn't pretty any damn way."

His erection didn't listen. He ignored it and fell asleep to dream about tall ladies with green eyes and red nun's habits. His tired mind had to make up most of the details under that red habit. But he almost had a wet dream anyway.

The sun was shining when Captain Gringo woke up, feeling a little better. He felt a *lot* better when he saw someone had draped his shoulder rig over his shirt and placed a fresh box of .38 ammo on his pants. He got up and dressed, sliding the gun on after checking it, and son of a bitch if it wasn't cleaned, loaded, and nobody had played funny funny with the mechanism.

Some sneak had been listening at the door, it seemed. For he'd just gotten himself put together when the door opened and yet another Sister of Santaria, this one in a pale lavender habit, brought a breakfast tray in. She wasn't bad-looking. He asked if she put out and she said if he wanted her he could have her. He passed it off as a joke. She wasn't *that* good-looking, and a guy needed his strength if he expected to run far in the near future.

He finished the hearty peon breakfast of refritos, rice, and tortillas with coffee strong enough to remove paint. Then he tested the door to see if he was locked in. He wasn't. He eased out into the corridor, wondered where the hell he thought he was going, and let out a yell. The one in lavender came to see what he wanted, looking sort of hopeful. He said he wanted to see Gaston. So she shrugged and led him to a nearby cell, where he found Gaston sitting up in bed, holding hands with yet another Sister of Santaria. She was a pretty little Mestiza. Gaston said, "Ah, there you are, my son. I seem to have died and gone to heaven, but I can't get this angel to climb in bed with me. She keeps saying something about my skull being cracked or something."

Captain Gringo laughed and said, "Your skull was cracked when I met you. But take it easy, Gaston. You had a serious concussion and those things can repeat on you if you move your head the wrong way for a few days."

"Merde alors, it is my adorable derriere I was thinking of moving the most, if only this child wasn't so stubborn. Eh bien, would someone tell me what is going on around here, Dick? They dress like nuns, they look like nuns, but she said she'll give me some as soon as I'm feeling better."

Captain Gringo found a chair in a corner, sat down, and filled in Gaston to the extent he himself knew about the weird setup.

Gaston heard him out, then said, "I see no reason to dash off before we get to know these ladies better. I buy the story about them being pestered by guerrillas. Guerrillas pester everybody, and there are always rumors of old Jesuit gold connected with these half-ruined missions they left behind when the colonial authorities expelled the order."

Captain Gringo said, "This mission isn't one the Pope would approve of, these days. I don't recall anyone mentioning money, either. Even for dough, the game here's getting a little rich for my blood, Gaston. These cultists are in contact with the coastal tribes, even if they don't seem quite as bad as the Brits said they were. They're still pretty wild. They were banging drums and screwing under my window half the night."

"Sacrebleu, and you left me out? Hold your horses, as they say in your Yanqui drollness. Perhaps we should give

this place the old once-over before we romp off into le bon
Dieu knows what, hein?''

Captain Gringo saw Gaston wasn't going anywhere for a
while, despite his chipper talk. The old Frenchman was pale
as a baby's puke, and Captain Gringo didn't feel like doing
pushups himself. So when Sister Lilith stuck her head in to
say Mother Salome wanted him, Captain Gringo told Gaston
to hang in there and followed the black nun.

They didn't go to the mother superior's quarters this time.
Mother Salome was waiting in the cloister garden. He noticed
the garden grew a lot of herbs. Some probably medicinal.
Whatever they'd put in his spiked chocolate had been pretty
effective, he recalled.

Mother Salome dismissed Sister Lilith and led him out to
where a pony cart stood waiting. He helped her in and she
took the reins, saying, "I thought you might enjoy a tour of
my parish," as he sat across from her. She ignored him when
he asked if parish was what she called her voodoo domain.
She clucked the pony into motion and a pair of massive gates
ahead of them swung open on oiled hinges. You couldn't see
who was doing it. He imagined a certain amount of stage
magic had been built into the old mission by the original
builders. All missionaries, even real ones, used a little mumbo-
jumbo to impress the natives.

As they rode out across the neatly cultivated milpas surrounding the thick stone walls, Mother Salome said, "I know
the things you've heard about us, Ricardo. Feel free to ask
any of the people we pass if they have been oppressed by our
order.''

He said, "The ones under my window last night seemed
happy as hell. Do you hop 'em up on drugs or do they just rut
like that for the glory of God?''

She grimaced and said, "Don't be a hypocrite, Ricardo
Walker. You do not enjoy a reputation as a celibate, you
know.''

"Touché. On the other hand, I'm not wearing a clerical collar and I hardly ever screw in church!"

"I doubt anyone did, when the mission was run by the Jesuits. I don't believe some of the stories told by their enemies. But, as you know, the Spanish authorities expelled the Soldiers of Christ ages ago, leaving a great void in the lives of simple people who'd been hunting one another's heads a generation or two before."

"So, your order moved in to fill the void?"

"Exactly. Actually, our founders were medical missionaries. Dutch Reformed, I believe. They were doctors, not theologians. As you may have observed, these natives can only absorb a few rudiments of Christianity. We manage to keep them more or less to the more important commandments, while indulging their tastes for the dramatic."

"I see you've dropped the Seventh Commandment."

She shrugged and said, "Their pagan religion was a fertility cult. We worry more about their physical well-being than their morals. But we have managed to stop a lot of tribal warfare, infanticide, and so on."

He frowned as he stared beyond her to some healthy-looking naked native kids cultivating yams in a well-tended milpa. He asked, "Are you saying all this Santaria stuff is a facade for a Dutch Protestant social program?"

She smiled softly and said, "My remote ancestors may have been Calvinists, Ricardo. I suppose at best I am an agnostic. Santaria is a little hard to fully accept if one knows how to read and write, no?"

"Don't look at me. You're the lady dressed up as some spooky kind of nun! Do you really have to go through all this nonsense just to keep them from eating one another, and, by the way, what's in all this for you, Salome?"

She shrugged and said, "I sometimes wonder about that myself. Perhaps I follow a higher calling than mythology of any variety. Perhaps it is simply inertia. You see, my mother was Mother Salome, as was her mother before her. So . . ."

"Gotcha," he cut in, adding, "That explains the mysterious immortal mother superior. I know this is no business of mine, but as long as we're clearing up mysteries, how do you Sisters of Santaria manage to descend from each other, if it's safe to assume you don't go in for miracles in mangers at least once in a while?"

She looked away and said, "We are not a celibate order. I'm not sure when the original medical mission workers adopted these quasi-Catholic habits, but it must have been while the Spanish still ruled here. They were as disapproving of Protestants as they were the Jesuits, so . . ."

"Right. What provincial religious fanatic is going to get off his fat siesta to investigate the distant doings of seeming nuns, as long as they're not Jesuits telling him he's naughty to keep Indian slave girls? How did the voodoo creep in?"

"Osmosis. The object was to keep the semipagan Indians and runaway African slaves healthy and reasonably prosperous. As I said, we don't allow blood sacrifice or any of the other more savage trimmings of Santaria. As long as a peon follows the golden rule and practices good hygiene, we must allow for harmless fun. I don't think God, if there is a God, cares whether people call him Dios, Jehova, Eli, Allah, or Mambo Jumbo, do you?"

"It's His problem. Can we head back now? It's getting hot and I can see I'm not going to see any children being burned on the altar of Moloch around here, Salome. I don't know if I approve of your charade or not, but it seems reasonably harmless."

She swung the pony around, but reined in when she saw a rider coming their way at full gallop. The cotton-clad peon slid his crowbait pony to a stop and called out, "Madre Salome! Soldados! Many soldados! Coming from the north! Hurry, Madre Salome! You must get back inside the walls of your mission poco tiempo!"

Captain Gringo stopped her from clucking their pony into motion and asked the rider how many and how far. He answered, "A whole column of infantry, señor! They fly the banner of León. But there are no Granada troops near here and they have already started helping themselves to chickens up the valley. Get Madre Salome safely away and we shall do our best to hold them off!"

"Good intentions, muchacho. wrong thinking. If those are the freelance soldados I think they are, they'll chop you up pronto. Ride back and tell your people to either run for the jungle or the mission. Don't try to fight them in the open. Those rifles they have are repeaters, and a .30-30 carries a killing kilometer or more!"

The peon spun his pony to ride back the way he had come. Captain Gringo took the reins from Mother Salome and said, "Let me show you how to drive this thing."

As he whipped the reins on the pony's rump, Mother Salome asked, "Can we count on you to defend us, Ricardo?"

He grimaced and didn't answer. He didn't know about defending this weird setup, but he sure was fond of his own and Gaston's asses!

Gaston was up when they got back. The Frenchman agreed a long siege would be a needless delay in their trip to Costa Rica. So the two soldiers of fortune went to work. The Sisters of Santaria had a well-stocked armory in the cellar. But most of the guns were antiques and Gaston just snorted when one of the nuns showed him some old brass cannon the Jesuits had left behind. He said the black powder on hand might serve to throw a stone ball a reasonable distance at a stationary target, if the ancient guns didn't blow up in one's face. But infantry didn't stay put. So Gaston supervised the mount-

162

ing of the Maxim gun on the highest tower of the mission complex, as the stronger Captain Gringo went to work outside the walls with a spade and some helpful peones.

The mysterious invaders took their time, enjoying roast chicken and such peon women as they could catch, no doubt. It was late afternoon by the time they marched on the mission, approaching via the only route to the almost fully moated mission in its oxbow. By then, of course, Captain Gringo had completed his preparations on the narrow strip of the landward approaches, sent peon runners out to organize the surrounding country, and climbed up to the tower to join Gaston and the machine gun.

Mother Salome had wanted to confront the troops, but they'd told her not to be silly and sent her below with the other nuns. So Captain Gringo was the guy to talk to when the khaki-clad mob of about sixty or more stopped outside rifle range, stared at the closed gates of the mission for a while, and sent a parley team in under a white flag and the León battle flag, flown upside down for some reason.

As they moved within conversation range, Captain Gringo called down, "That's close enough. Who are you and what do you want?"

A fat greasy man wearing an officer's cap and smoking a big cigar called back, "We are the army of the great general, El Venganzadero! For why have you locked us out, my friend?"

Gaston muttered, "They're not León regulars. Commisioned officers don't assume dramatique nicknames."

Captain Gringo nodded and muttered, "Light the fuse and let me stall the prick." Then he called out, "We lock the gates at night as a precaution against ladrónes, lieutenant. It is said some sons of bitches have been stealing chickens around here."

"I spit on your chickens! I am no lieutenant! Can you not

see I am a major? Open the damned gates. We are on a mission of vengeance, but we are most tired and need a place for to rest awhile. Is it true that is a convent you are perched upon, my friend? Hey, what are you, a priest?''

"You might call me an undertaker, major. What's this mission of revenge you guys are on?"

"It is not important to you, funny man. Just some dirty double-dealers who sent us some faulty goods for our hard-won gold. Open that damn gate and let us see if the sisters in there are pretty, no?"

"They're very pretty. But you can't peek. If I were you I'd march on, major."

"Hey, is that any way to talk? I don't think you like us, eh? You know what happens if you don't open that gate, and muy pronto?"

"Let me guess. You'll huff and you'll puff and you'll blow our house down? Take a hike, muchacho. You've got nothing we want and you can't have what we've got!"

The dumpy warlord consulted with his fellows, shook his fist up at them, and called out, "You asked for it, funny man! Now you're going to get it!"

He started back for his own lines.

He didn't get there. As the quick fuse and its buried branches did their job, dynamite charges started going off right where Captain Gringo had planted them. He'd figured they'd line up across the neck of land just out of small-arms range. So a lot of his work was done for him right off, as khaki-clad figures, or parts of them, flew skyward on gouts of flame and brick-red soil!

Those who didn't happen to be standing right over a charge did what anyone but possibly well-trained troops would have done. They got the hell away from the staggered explosions. Since Captain Gringo had timed and placed his dynamite with forethought, the survivors ran his way, into machine-gun range. He grinned, held his fire until his nearest targets were almost close enough that he could depress the Maxim without exposing himself dangerously, and gave them a full belt at point-blank traverse!

Most of them went down like good little guerrillas before Gaston had to change the belt for him. When he opened up again, he chopped hell out of those still on their feet and running the other way. Some few made it through the haze of red dust over the row of dynamite craters. It didn't do them much good. The peones dedicated to the mission rose out of the corn beyond with wicked grins and gleaming machetes. Gaston put a mocking hand to his face and said, "Oh, it's too awful, I can't look!"

It *was* sort of gruesome, by the time the last of the bastards had been cut down. But that wasn't what was bothering Captain Gringo. He levered the action again, swore, and said, "That was close. This fucking gun is shot. The operating rod is busted in two. I sure hope that's the end of this shit. Because we don't have a machine gun anymore, old buddy!"

The local natives enjoyed the victory celebration more than Captain Gringo did. Although since Gaston jumped into the orgy he could be said to be at least in a more relaxed mood. Captain Gringo was more interested in his broken operating rod. As he rummaged around in the cellar workshop for a steel rod that looked anything like the broken part, Mother Salome joined him, asking what he was doing down here.

He explained, "Thanks to everyone in Nicaragua apparently patronizing the same gun runners, we've got all the .30-30 rounds a busy machine gunner might use up in a dozen skirmishes like today's. But thanks to your rusty climate, this Maxim now fires single fire, if at all. I could do better with any of those rifles we salvaged this evening. But rifle fire isn't as convincing an argument, even from behind these thick stone walls. Don't you buy any agricultural machinery at all, Salome? All I need is one lousy steel rod I could maybe whittle to fit. That's if you had a decent rat-tail file, which I can't seem to find either!''

She said, ''Our flock has always gotten by with simple farm tools, I'm afraid, Ricardo.''

''You ain't as afraid as me, Salome. If another bunch like that last one shows up, we're in trouble! Listen, are you sure you wouldn't like Costa Rica? This situation is getting grim, Salome. For some reason, a mess of guerrillas all seem interested in this area at once. I think I smell some kind of double-cross in the air. Would you tell me one thing, for cross-your-heart true? It's important.''

''What is it you suspect us of now, Ricardo? I assure you we have not taken sides in the civil war.''

''Sure, sure, the twentieth century is peering over the horizon at us and you expect to go on living here in the Middle Ages. What I really want to know, no bull, is have you girls been selling arms to sort of keep the church fund solvent?''

''Good Lord, where would we get arms to sell, Ricardo?''

He thought and said, ''I'll buy that. A lady gunrunner using a convent for a front would have to be a little closer to salt water. But someone close must be shipping the stuff in wholesale. That fat boy who wanted to find out if it was true what they said about convent girls mentioned he'd been sold some faulty merchandise. I noticed at the British post that ammo corrodes in this climate if you don't keep an eye on it. Those guys who split my scalp with a .30-30 round were from another band, and coming from the south. But they packed the same name brands, too. It sort of makes one wonder about someone's business ethics.''

''What has all this arms smuggling to do with us, Ricardo?''

''Not much, if I take your word for it. But this mission is in a battle zone indeed, now. The *nice* soldiers are over to the west. Browned-off guerrillas ain't nice. They figure to be coming at us from all directions, and, as you see, I just lost my most persuasive argument.''

''But what can we do, Ricardo? We have no choice but to stand our ground and hope these walls are strong enough, no?''

''No. I could tell you about some guys who tried that at another mission called the Alamo, but it's a boring story. You don't try to hold a static position if there's anywhere to run to, Salome. Once you're surrounded, you're committed for keeps. Meanwhile, there's miles and miles of nothing in every direction. You can pick the direction. Just so it's out of this death trap.''

''We can't abandon the mission, Ricardo! It's all we've worked for, for so long!''

''Nuts, kiddo. How long into the twentieth century do you figure to maintain this relic of the Dark Ages? For God's sake, the *National Geographic* will be taking pictures of your quaint natives as soon as it's safe to travel down here again! Give it up, Salome. You're a nice-looking dame, and this is a thankless task at best. Let whoever wins the war worry about the natives. Hardly anyone burns pagans at the stake anymore. Your ancestors have already turned them into reasonable facsimiles of your average downtrodden peasant. What are you trying to prove, that you look good in red?''

She started to cry. He took her in his arms and said, ''Oh, hell, let's not blubber about it! I'll tell you what, Salome. Let Gaston and me lead just you and your sisters to some halfway safe place. You can come back and play weird when the fighting dies down. If you stay here, you'll just wind up gang-raped or worse, and what good will that do anyone?''

''But my poor peones!'' she sobbed. So he shook her, kissed her, and insisted, ''They're not *your* peones. They're grown men and women who can duck out of sight good. I watched 'em do it today. Leave the gates open. Bury all the treasures, if you have any, and what can passing guerrillas do, write dirty words on the walls? The place is fireproof, and no bandito has the ambition to go into the demolition business for free. You and your girls are the honey that's drawing the flies here, Salome. Get out of this trap and there's no bait. Hell, your peones will be *safer* with you out of the area, see?"

She said, "I have to think about it, Ricardo. Ah, would you mind kissing me again? I somehow find it very comforting to be held in your strong arms and kissed like a little girl."

He did as she asked, but Mother Salome was no little girl. She was one big dame, and built sort of interesting under that dumb red habit. She didn't kiss like a little girl, either. She kissed like what she was, a member of a noncelibate order who hadn't been getting any lately. He didn't want to know who'd kissed her last, so he didn't ask. He was no angel, either, even if he was kissing a nun.

As he warmed to comforting her and felt her big breasts, too, she protested, "Stop that, Ricardo. Who ever heard of making love to the mother superior in the cellar?"

He kissed her again and asked where guys were supposed to make love to mother superiors. So she led him upstairs and they locked themselves in her quarters to do it right.

She peeled out of her red robe and hood before he even had his gun rig off, and leaped coyly into the four-poster. There was a lot of coy to leap, once he saw her in what she wore under her red habit, which was nothing.

Salome was a big green-eyed blonde. Repeat big. She had to weigh close to 160, but as she lay face down on the bedclothes, trembling with embarrassment, impatience, or both, he saw her weight was nicely distributed under her ivory-white soft skin. He slid in beside her, rolled her over, and kissed her right with her heroic breasts flattened against his heaving chest and a big heavy thigh raised over his hips as she thrust her blond bush against his questing erection. As he rolled her on her back to mount her properly, she needed no pillow under her substantial, derriere to present herself at the perfect angle to him. As he entered her, she gasped and said, "Oh, wait, I fear you're much too big for me!"

That wasn't as funny as it sounded, coming from a dame who could have wrestled professionally. She was tight as hell for such a big blond broad.

He settled his weight on her gently. None of the rest of him made much impression on a girl her size. He kissed her frightened tears away as she kept her eyes closed and pleaded with him to snuff out the lights. He wasn't about to dismount and start all over again. For if she ever crossed those big legs it would take the dynamite he no longer had to part them against her will. He started moving gently, trying to keep from going nuts in the tempting contrast of her heroic white curves after not having had a woman for a while, and that one a tiny dark squaw in the dark. As she began to respond, she sniffed that he mustn't look at her because he might think she was too fat. He promised to keep his eyes closed, too, as he moved up higher, started moving faster, and thoroughly enjoyed the view. She wasn't too fat. She hourglassed better than Lillian Russel in the *Police Gazette*, and she wasn't wearing those pink tights.

She reached up to hug him to her big smooth sofa pillows as she spread her big thighs wider and started moving to help. It helped a lot. Even feeling still a bit weak from the loss of blood the day before, he found himself pounding hot and heavy. She was doing most of the work now.

She moaned in passion, raised her knees until they were braced against his shoulders, and now she was doing all the work as she bounced him almost out of her with each upstroke. He came in her, hard, and went limp atop her, but she hardly noticed as she gave him the ride of his life while he simply relaxed and enjoyed it. For a while. In anything that nice, a man could hardly stay detached long. As she stiffened in orgasm and threw her legs wide, it was his turn to move hot and fast. She gasped, "Oh, God, it's so good I can't stand it, Ricardo! Stop just a minute and let me gather my wits again! You have me so sensitized it's driving me crazy, and if you don't stop I'll . . . Never mind what I just said, darling! Do it! Do it! Do it and never stop doing it!"

He had to, of course, after he'd exploded in her again. But not before she'd enjoyed another long shuddering orgasm so they could go limp together with his bare rump a good foot above the mattress as she milked him with her pulsating tight wetness. After a time she felt it rising to the occasion again inside her and pleaded, "Can't we have the lights out, darling? I feel so . . . naked with the lights on."

He'd thought that was the general idea, but he rolled off long enough to snuff the candle wicks and climb back in. He was missing a very large female, it seemed, until she giggled in the dark and reached out to grab his semierection, which didn't stay that way long, and said, "I want to get on top now. I could never do that with you watching me."

He let her. As she settled her considerable weight on him and began to move up and down on his shaft, he grasped what she meant and repressed a chuckle at the mental picture she presented when her big breasts started pillow fighting with his face. He inhaled a turgid nipple and kept it in his mouth with no effort despite her bounces. They were nicely formed as well as big, but there was plenty of slack built in. He reached down between them and played with her clit as she slid up and down his shaft. It inspired her to new heights. She rose so high she lost it and would have ruined him forever when she sat back down on it if there hadn't been another place for it to go. She gasped, "Oh, my God! Do you know where you just stuck that monster" but kept moving, inspired by his massaging fingers, as he said, "I didn't do it. You did. Does it hurt?"

"Yes. I mean no. I mean . . . could you move your hand faster, darling?"

So he did, and they enjoyed it that way, too. So much so that she asked him to Greek her right. He helped her get into position on her hands and knees and did his best to please. Her big behind felt different than Rubia's as he held the cheeks apart and gave her the full length up her rear in long hard strokes, knowing it was hard to hurt a big strong dame like her no matter what he did to her. She giggled and said, "Ooh, that's terribly naughty. I like it that way, but save it and shoot our baby into me right!"

He didn't stop. He couldn't have. But that remark inspired him about as much as an ice-water enema. So he asked, in a desperately casual tone, "Uh, didn't you have any, well, precautions in mind, doll?"

She said, "No. I told you how we Sisters of Santaria reproduced. My mother had me by a traveling Indian trader, I think. Why?"

"Your mother must have been very blond indeed. Uh, don't take this personal, Salome, but I'm sort of reluctant to leave kids I'll never get to know behind me in my travels."

"Oh, don't worry, darling. If it's a boy I'll make him a sexton. If it's a girl, of course, she'll someday take my place as the eternal Mother Salome."

He didn't answer. He was coming, damn it. But he could see his arguments for leaving the mission to the guerrillas and other pests had made no impression at all on the big blond beautiful dumb broad!

Gaston was all for pushing on when they met after breakfasts in bed the next morning. Gaston had spent the night with the dusky Sister Lilith. But he said he'd be able to walk by noon, probably. As they strolled alone in the cloister garden, Gaston took something from his pocket and handed it over, adding, "Read the lettering on this ammo box and tell me we should linger in these interesting but très strange parts, Dick."

Captain Gringo read the white lettering on blue that some-one had tried to cover with indelible pencil and almost succeeded, but for the damp heat the cartridge box had been subjected to in an unfortunate guerrilla's pants.

The box had been manufactured by Woodbine Arms, Ltd. U.K.

Captain Gringo whistled and said, "So, our old pal, Sir Basil Hakim, the Merchant of Death, has been shipping arms and ammo to these parts, eh?"

Gaston said, "Oui, doubtless to both sides, if I know that degenerate Anglo-Turkish arms monger. The .30-30 rounds are Chinese Copies of Yanqui ammo, but made in England, Hong Kong, or who knows, by the busy little fingers of that très crooked old rascal. Since I found this in the trash, left when the adorable sisters reloaded your ammo belt, I have had a jolly time remembering some of the droll pranks that triple-titted son of a harelipped whore and a double-donged camel has played on people in the past. Do you recall that other time we met some ladies who were supposed to be nuns, Dick? The ones who turned out to be agents of Sir Basil Hakim?"

"Oh boy! They were convincing as *real* nuns, too! Hmm, could be, Gaston. But I can't see Salome working for Basil Hakim. For one thing, she's not bright enough. For another, what would he set up here for? We're way the hell inland. He runs his guns in off that fleet of ships he owns. Also, leave us not forget this odd mission was established long before even that old bastard could have been born."

He handed the possible clue back, shook his head, and said, "Makes more sense they ran the stuff ashore at that fishing village, like we thought. Those guys were pissed about someone selling them bad ammo. I'm pissed at the way that Maxim fell apart on me after a few modest bursts of fire, and we took it off guys at that same fishing village. You know our friendly neighborhood Merchant of Death likes to unload factory seconds and condemned ammunition on the sucker in bananaland. The Prince of Wales would never swap dates with him if Hakim ever pulled shit like that in the British military. Hold it, I just had a brilliant thought!''

"May we listen in, oh mighty thinker of mine?"

"Sure. It works. Woodbine Arms, Limited, sells to everybody, undercutting on prices because Hakim doesn't bother paying, half the time. All this surplus .30-30 showing up down here must have originally been ordered by the U.S. Army. Our ordnance officers aren't as dumb as illiterate warlords. So they'd naturally reject ammo that was bent, split, or missing its primers. Hakim would never pay to have it shipped back across the Atlantic. Who the hell could he sucker with it? Sure, he shipped a cargo of defective or at least unreliable .30-30 down here to unload on the bush-leaguers.''

Gaston frowned and objected, "Some of the .30-30 we've been shooting people with seems to work well enough, Dick.''

Captain Gringo said, "Sure. Most of it was good stuff, issued us by the British constabulary. What we've salvaged since has been okay rounds culled from boxes and boxes of half-rotten brass by very very pissed-off guys. When a ordnance man spots one or two bad rounds in a box, he tends to reject the whole box. It would cost Hakim more to sort all the rejected shipment for total shit than it would to just reseal the boxes, mark out his own trademark, and sell it for what he could get to anyone dumb enough to pay.''

Gaston nodded and said, "Eh bien, that solves part of the mystery. I leave the rest for the no-doubt outraged customers of Woodbine Arms to sort out for themselves, hein? We are not making anything on the deal and I would like to get out of here before I have to nibble that Sister Lilith again. She gives très delightful head, but she has much to learn about feminine hygiene!''

Captain Gringo agreed, and they would have left during the siesta hour, when tedious good-byes could be avoided and nobody would notice which way they'd gone. But as they were planning what to take with them, a rider came in, making like Paul Revere in Spanish, to stir everybody up with the news that this time someone was coming from the *south*. Not in the mufti of banditos, not in the quasi-uniform of some private warlord, but aboard a steamboat, with a four-incher mounted on its foredeck!

Captain Gringo and Gaston didn't waste time running topside to gape down the river at the impossible sight. The nuns said no steamboat had ever come up their river before, with or without a deck gun. The two soldiers of fortune didn't think the scout who'd ridden in looked like a lunatic who couldn't tell a steamboat from an alligator, and they knew that they had to do something about it long before it got within sight of the walls. A four-incher could lob a shell, high explosive, a good three miles with deadly precision!

With the help of some peones and a couple of strong sisters, they dragged the abandoned Spanish cannon outside and set them up in the open, so Gaston could at least aim elevated fire. He had no idea whether they'd blow up or not when and if he fired them. They had to do something poco tiempo.

The old gun carriages were rotted half to punk and the guns wouldn't elevate to forty-five aboard them anyway. So the first thing Gaston ordered were some holes in the red clay, with roughly forty-five-degree slopes aimed downriver. Then he gathered barrel staves, blocks of wood, rags, and anything else he could use as improvised wedging. As they worked, Mother Salome came out to ask if there was anything she could do. Captain Gringo said, "Yeah, doll. Leave us some workmen as powder monkeys. Then herd you and your sisters at least five miles up the valley. You should be safe where we turned around yesterday."

"But, Ricardo, what about my mission?"

"That's why we're setting up out here. They'll probably lob the first shells inside the walls to blow hell out of anybody dumb enough to stay inside. Then they'll land and send riflemen in to mop up as they just keep the incoming mail coming!"

"But, Ricardo, we have many rifles and much ammunition. Would not it be possible to defend ourselves as these walls were intended to be defended?"

"Honey, the old seventeenth-century Soldados de Cristo who shoved all the brittle masonry up in the sky had nothing like modern four-inchers in mind. The walls might stand up to old-fashioned cannonballs. I know they could take all the poison darts and arrows the Jesuits had to worry about. But . . . Look, will you gather the girls and haul your pretty asses? If we manage to at least scare them enough to matter, you can all come back and hold black Mass all you like. Right now your mission's an obvious target and a certain death trap! How are you coming with the elevation down there, Gaston?"

Gaston said, "Très lousy. I believe I have the line of sight. The elevation? Merde alors! If there was time to zero on my two target points, I could try various charges to see which one drops what where. You see, forty-five is maximum range if one uses these antiques as mortars, as I must. But too vast a charge will send the projectile over, while too small a charge . . ."

"I know how to zero a mortar, damn it! What do you intend to fire *out* at them?"

"Cans of chili sauce. They had a case of them in the kitchen and they fit the bore, by sheer good chance."

"Oh for God's sake, Gaston. Chili sauce?"

"I find it a droll suggestion too. But the old gunners left no old cannonballs, and to go anywhere, a projectile must fit the bore, non? We have plenty of black powder and plenty of cans. I've no idea what the results might be. But one does one's best with what is on hand, non?"

Captain Gringo saw Mother Salome was still standing there. He said, "Damn it, Salome! If you don't move it I'll . . . I'll make you do it with the lights on!"

That seemed to work. Salome ran into the mission, calling out to the other Sisters of Santaria as Captain Gringo hunkered down by Gaston's nearest gun emplacement, squinted south, and said, "Okay, what's your point of aim, Chef Gaston?"

The Frenchman said, "Both curves of the second oxbow down there. One cannot see far from ground level, but fortunately the level is nice and flat, hein? I shall open fire as they round the far bend. If I miss and they persist, my second great gun is zeroed in on the next bend, where they will present a seemingly stationary target for the moment as they swing to face this way. As you see, I have prepared charges of various weights, wrapped in those droll silk kerchiefs. Silk burns poof, with the powder, so one may get off better than a round a minute with my considerable mais reckless skill. I shall never speak to you again if either of these barrels burst, but with luck, I hope to lob at least a few cans of chili into them, non?"

Captain Gringo had to laugh, despite the danger he foresaw no matter what the results of Gaston's experiment. He stared down the river and said, "Okay, we give it our best shot. When they round that last bend, we run like hell. What do you think, zigzagging up slope for the treeline?"

"Better than ducking behind the mission, where they are certain to be dropping long rounds. Ah, I see we have visitors!"

Captain Gringo saw the smoke plume too. He nodded and said, "Yeah, they're boiling upstream with a bone in their teeth. Where the hell do you suppose that steamboat *came* from, Gaston?"

Gaston said, "How should I know? I don't know where that river runs to. Obviously *they* do. You had better take cover, my child. Chef Gaston is about to mix some chili sauce, hein?"

Captain Gringo turned and told the nearby peon helpers to start running and stay that way until they were out of range. They needed no convincing. But just in case they had, they'd barely started running when a dull distant thud sounded in the still valley air and something came screaming through the sky their way!

Gaston sneered, "Merde, they are way over," as the first shell hit with a louder roar on the far side of the mission. Captain Gringo instinctively glanced that way. He spotted the red habit of Mother Salome in the open gateway. What in the hell was she doing there? He yelled at her. She stood rooted in confusion as a second shell keened in to explode somewhere inside, tossing roof tiles like confetti against the blue sky. Captain Gringo swore and leaped up to run over and at least make her hit the dirt.

Before he could reach her, she was outlined from behind in orange as a shell exploded in the courtyard behind her! She flew out the gateway like a cork from a warm bottle of champagne, turning a cartwheel in the air as she shed her red nun's habit and landed flat and nude in the dust. Too flat and nude for such a big dame. As he dropped to his knees by her, he saw her whole skull had been blown out of her head by a shard of shrapnel, leaving her oddly still-pretty face a flat mask on the sticky red clay!

Her other bone structure had simply been shattered like glass inside her dead naked body. He gagged, turned away, and started crawling, as yet another shell hit the mission wall to bore through before it detonated inside, blowing tiles and timber in every direction. He kept crawling, sobbing, "Damm it, Gaston! What are you waiting for!"

Gaston didn't answer as he hunkered between the two ancient brass cannon. Then, as Captain Gringo was saying very rude things about his mother, Gaston touched off the first one with the tip of his cigar.

The old cannon belched a vast cloud of white black-powder smoke. The old brass held, but nothing seemed to happen for a very long time. Then a pretty good geyser of white water spouted ahead of the flat-bottomed steamboat's bows. If it impressed the khaki-clad crew manning the deck gun, it didn't stop them from ranging on Gaston's smoke, or the steamboat from pressing on around the bend. Gaston sighed and said, "I was short. But now at least I know my point of aim with that one. Let's see if I have the upstream point properly zeroed, hein?"

He waited, waited, until the steamboat swung around the bend and, as he'd foretold, seemed to hang motionless in the current for a few moments. Captain Gringo muttered, "Oh, shit," and started firing with his Krag.

The results surprised everyone on both sides. Captain Gringo *dropped* one of the bastards as their shell skimmed over him and Gaston!

Then Gaston's can of chili sauce exploded with surprising noise on the flat deck by the gun. Captain Gringo worked the Krag's bolt and fired round after round, hoping at least to hit the fucking boat at this range. Gaston laughed and re-charged his own weapon to fire more chili at them, now that he had them ranged. Captain Gringo did even better. By sheer luck he hit one of the four-inch shells the bewildered gunners had dropped as they scattered, bewildered at the hot chili sauce and wondering how in hell *that* had happened.

The four-incher exploded, blowing men overboard or drop-ping them to the deck with agonizing shrapnel wounds. Then another can of chili sauce burst among them to cause more confusion and even louder screams as the hot sauce splashed over bleeding flesh! The boat turned broadside. Gaston laughed and said, ''What, you do not like my cooking?'' and lobbed another can through the pilothouse window.

The two soldiers of fortune couldn't see what was happen-ing inside, but it must have discouraged hell out of the men at the helm. The steamer swung its rear paddle wheel their way and proceeded to churn up white water as it headed back downstream at full steam.

Gaston added one last kick in the ass as they passed through his downstream aiming point. Now that he had the range, the skilled old artillery ace lobbed a can of chili into the wooden paddles. This time the can didn't burst. It snapped at least two paddles. As they limped out of range at full steam but reduced speed, Gaston said, ''Perhaps, next time, a little more salt, non? They can get downstream, with the current's help. I doubt they shall be coming *upstream* for some time, hein?''

A couple of the other Sisters of Santaria, including Lilith, had managed to get themselves killed by staying too long in the mission to gather belongings they no longer needed. The only death that really confused the natives was that of their mother superior. As Captain Gringo and Gaston gathered supplies from amid the wreckage, a dele-gation led by the local alcalde timidly approached them, hats in hands, to ask for religious guidance. The alcalde said, ''We do not understand, señores. Mother Salome was supposed to be immortal!''

Captain Gringo said, ''Yeah, well, wait around three days

and something may work out. Meanwhile, if you want some last advice on hygiene, bury the dead and distribute the supplies and tools in this shell among the living.''

"But what is to become of us, señores? We have never had to concern ourselves with our futures. The kind Sisters of Santaria did all our thinking for us.''

Captain Gringo nodded gently and said, "Those were the good old days, Señor Alcalde. We live in changing times. Someday when the civil war is over, someone is sure to ride in with all sorts of plans for your social advancement. Meanwhile, you have crops planted, your own roofs didn't get blown off, and, hell, it's time to grow up, muchachos! You've been taught how to speak Spanish and a smattering of semi-Christian customs. Just keep your pants on around official visitors and keep the drums down to a roar and you'll get by.''

"Will you not stay to be our leader, señor? We will do anything you say. You can have all the food, pulque, and women a man could wish for.''

"Thanks, but no thanks, Señor Alcalde. We're doing you a favor by moving on. Just go back to growing corn and beans, duck when you see anyone who wants to liberate you, and you'll be better off than before. I'd stay away from this ruin if I were you. Someone wanted it, or wanted it wrecked. I don't know why, either, but they may be back. Let them have it. There's nothing worth fighting for here, now.''

The alcalde gave a defeated little sigh. Captain Gringo nodded and said, "You'll get used to thinking, after a while. Could any of you tell us where that river leads? We don't want to wind up anywhere near that steamboat again.''

The peones consulted one another. Finally one said, "It goes nowhere, señor. The steamboat must have been a curse sent by the elder gods. The river comes from nowhere in the jungles to the west. It goes nowhere into the jungles to the east, after passing through another water gap in the ridge over that way."

A brighter-looking man said, "Idioso! Every river must drain somewhere. Otherwise this valley would be a lake, no?"

A third, older peon said, "I have heard it said the river ends in the great black-water swamps far to the east. I have no idea how they came out of there with a steamboat. Nobody lives in the black-water swamp but Mosquito Indians. I don't think los Mosquitoes know how to make a steamboat."

Captain Gringo nodded grimly and said, "Bueno. Now I have one more favor to ask of you, Señor Alcalde. My comrade and me need a boat. A dugout canoe will do."

The alcalde said that was easy. As they went to find a canoe, Gaston asked, "Dick, have you gone mad? You just said we wanted no more to do with that mysterious steamboat and its murderous crew!"

Captain Gringo nodded and said, "That was before I figured out who the pricks were. I took them for some half-ass Nicaraguan soldiery."

"I saw the khaki too. Am I supposed to guess the rest, or do you feel up to letting me in on it, you stern-faced growler of growls?"

"Was I growling? Yeah, I am pretty pissed off. Salome was a nice dame. It's obvious who ran that tub up here to set up a new distribution point. Do you know any gunrunner but that goddamn Basil Hakim who can afford his own private navy?"

Gaston blinked and said, "Ah, the light dawns. Oui, the detestable toad of a Turk is dumping semiworthless merchandise on both sides in the endless civil war. The mother-sodomizing arms merchant would rather peddle his toys closer to the war zone. The child-molesting destroyer of perfectly good ass sent his hired thugs to do the deed, and one must say they seem to have done it! But before we scamper for the east coast again, my avenger of ladies in red, how do we get *off* said coast once we do some dreadful thing to dear Sir Basil, hein?"

"Easy. First we go back to that constabulary post and pick up our safe-conduct passes from that dopey major and his wise-ass junior, MacLean. Then, with that in our pockets, we seek out and destroy Hakim, or at least his local agents. I'm hoping Hakim himself will be in Greytown. He's not about to risk his degenerate carcass in any jungle when guys like us hire out so cheap."

"True. I recall the disgusting little toad's très luxurious private yacht. I would not leave it to leap into any leech-infested swamps if I owned a floating harem either. But how are we to get those safe-conduct papers even from a halfwit like Major Chalmers? The deal was for us to lead an expedition here and wipe this mission out, not to make friends with the astonishingly sexy Sisters of Santaria!"

"Hey, do you kiss and tell, Gaston? I don't. The deal was that we got safe conduct to Greytown and a no-questions boat out, after the mission had been put out of business. So it's out of business, as those Indian scouts skulking about will no doubt tell the constabulary pretty soon now. What do you want, egg in your beer?"

Gaston laughed wildly and said, "Sacrebleu, I have created a monster! You were such a nice boy when first we met. Now you are a bigger rogue than me! Kiss me, you fool, it ought to work!"

They should have walked. The unmapped river indeed took them through the water gap through the eastern ridge that had blocked their earlier passage south. Then they got lost in the vast black-water swamps between the rise and the coastal cuestas. They'd loaded the dugout with enough food to last a couple of weeks. They wound up eating all of it as they paddled into endless blind alleyways. They saw no sign of the mysterious steamboat. Which was just as well. They had two rifles, their pistols, and half the time they took a pot shot at something edible in the soggy waste the cartridge was a dud. Even culled over, the ammo the pissed-off irregulars had been packing was something to get pissed off about. The primers had either corroded in the damp heat or never been properly manufactured in the first place.

They gave up on where the steamboat might have gone. The choices of channels were endless. When Captain Gringo spotted a trail blaze on a tree dominating an eastbound channel, they paddled that way, and two weeks after leaving the ruined mission, they grounded the prow of the now-empty and waterlogged canoe on the trail leading back to the constabulary post. Hiking on in was a relief to their cramped legs and only took until sunset.

They made it as the gates were about to close. Gaston went to see if any food or women were left at the campsite between the school and base hospital. Captain Gringo handed him his rifle and went to check in at G.H.Q.

Major Chalmers was just locking his office for the day. He was already well on his way to dead drunk and it took a while to get him to remember who Captain Gringo was. As they stood on the veranda, Chalmers said, "Ah, yes, chaps who went to do something about those cultists, what? You'd best report to MacLean when he gets back. On patrol at the moment. Should be back in a day or so, eh what?"

Captain Gringo growled, "We don't have a day or so, major. We did the job you sent us to do. We want those safe-conduct passes you promised us."

Chalmers looked undecided, shrugged, and let the tall America in long enough to scrawl him a couple of notes that could have been Sanscrit, but on official-looking stationery. Captain Gringo was glad MacLean wasn't there. He didn't have to sell the dopey senior officer any bull. Chalmers apparently never considered that a gentleman might lie to him.

He handed the passes over and asked if he could go home now. Captain Gringo said, "One more favor and I'm out of your hair for good. We need a few days' rations and some decent ammo if we're to make it to Greytown. I know the trading post and armory are closed right now. But you must have keys and it'll only take a minute."

Chalmers blinked and said, "What? What? Keys you say? Right-ho, got 'em in this drawer. Here, you take what you like from stores and leave the keys with the gate guard when you leave. Got to have a lie-down, what? Heat's getting to me old noggin, I fear."

Captain Gringo didn't argue when things turned out too good to be true. He pocketed the keys and helped the major to his feet to send him on his tottering way. Then he crossed the compound to join Gaston and the adelitas around Gordita's fire, if that *was* Gordita!

He grinned at the Mestiza stirring a big pot of something that smelled great and asked, "Gordita, is that really you? You must have shed mucho pounds in the last few days!"

The no longer fat, albeit not exactly skinny, Gordita sighed and explained, "I have not been able to get one bite of chocolate in this horrid place. I thought I was going to die. But, in truth, I no longer seem to have such a craving."

"Don't ever crave it again. You're almost gorgeous with your skin cleared up and a waistline to call your own. What happened here? We seem to be missing some dames. Where's Lolita, Rubia, and that little Rosita?"

Gaston piped up, "I already have the story. Apparently Indian gossip encouraged some of the girls to make a run for home. The constabulary was mildly annoyed. So they haven't let these sweet things near the gates of late."

Captain Gringo said, "It's okay now. Got passes and a go-ahead from the CO. At the moment he's dead drunk and

MacLean is off somewhere. We'd better eat that yummy-smelling stuff and get going before the situation changes. It can't change for the better.''

They all hunkered around the pot and dug in. Captain Gringo was too hungry to complain, but he was mildly surprised at how bland the stew tasted after all. Gordita defended herself by explaining the horrid Anglos had refused to issue her all the seasoning she wanted. Captain Gringo ate just enough to stuff his gut and told the others to finish eating and pack while he helped himself to provisions from the trading post and armory.

They just managed. The tall American was back in no time, packing a gunnysack like Santa Claus and saying, "Okay, let's get out of here."

Gaston protested, "What is the hurry, Dick? We have bedding, a dry camp, and half-a-dozen ladies to entertain. Would not we be better off in daylight on the river to the coast?"

"No. We're not taking that river east of the post. Don't have a canoe now, and I don't like surprises in an overloaded dugout anyway. I know where we are. I had a good long look at the wall map in the office while that drunk was writing our passes. We'll leave via the south gate, follow the cuesta south till it's cut by the east-west Greytown road, and there we are. Come on, gang, get a *move* on!"

They did, protesting and bitching all the way out the south gate. Captain Gringo handed the guard on duty there the major's keys and told him to hang in there. He herded his party through the Mosquito Indian village and told Gaston to shut up when the Frenchman suggested paying a call to see if Barbara and Maria had made it home all right. Then he remembered his manners, and as they were passing the last hut in the village he ran over, yanked the door hangings aside, and told the old man screwing the little girl inside to get dressed, warn the other Indians, and run south like hell.

He didn't linger for further explanations. He rejoined Gaston and the six adelitas and said, "Pick 'em up and lay 'em down! We've got maybe three or four more minutes if I timed it right!"

Gaston fell in step beside him, gasping, "Slow down, you species of a big moose! What are we running from?"

"Bad guys. Jesus, Gaston, you're the guy who taught me this trade. Haven't you caught on yet?"

"Mais non, I can't run and think at the same time. Are you suggesting those constabulary troops have done something naughty?"

"They're not constabulary troops. They never were. I should have known Whitehall wouldn't pull a land grab as raw as that, after President Cleveland slapped their wrists with the Monroe Doctrine and U.S. Marines down in South America just a few months ago."

"Sacre goddamn, my suspicious youth, they certainly look like real constabulary. They act like real constabulary. Their uniforms. Their très convincing outpost . . ."

Right. They even have official stationery. Sir Basil Hakim manufactures supplies for the British military. Need I say more?"

"Mon Dieu! Are you suggesting this whole apparent British invasion is but a front for that double-dealing baby-raping arms merchant?"

"Ain't suggesting. Saying. I didn't know for sure until I tasted Gordita's bland stew back there. That's when I knew who sent that armed steamboat up the river. MacLean sent us as a feint, as we thought he might have. He knew it would take time to thread a steamboat through that maze of waterways, and meanwhile he hoped our half-ass overland march would keep all the Indian scouts occupied. We probably put MacLean and Sergeant Muldoon out of business with your chili sauce artillery. I know we spattered hell out of *some* of the wounded. You can still smell hot chili sauce near the base hospital. They must dump the dressings somewhere close."

Gaston laughed with delight and said, "Of course! I wondered why I did not taste the flavoring I smelled in adorable Gordita's très bland offering. Next time I say a can of chili sauce fits the bore, don't laugh at me!"

Captain Gringo had been keeping track of time and distance. He held up a hand and said, "Okay, gang, everyone fan out and hit the dirt. *Move,* damn it!"

The girls didn't hesitate once they saw Captain Gringo and Gaston hit the deck. Gaston said, "I suppose there's a reason for this. But you said the drunken major never suspected anything, Dick."

"What can I tell you? When you say a man's a drunk, you've said it all. He was probably bewildered and anxious to get rid of us as well as three sheets to the wind. He's not used to giving orders without Hakim's agent, MacLean, feeding him his acting lines. All they could know is that we went some damn where, and when they arrived, someone surprised hell out of 'em with artillery fire the mission wasn't supposed to have. By now they know the Sisters of Santaria are out of business, so what the hell, they were planning to move their base of operations closer to the war zone as soon as their wounded recovered."

Gaston nodded and said, "Oui, that is the style of that très sneaky Basil Hakim. Should anyone question British bases so deep in Nicaraguan territory, Whitehall, not the lovable drinking companion of the Prince of Wales, gets to explain it to Washington. By the time the flap is over, Hakim will have made a killing in the sale of semi-useless arms, and that, as they say, will be that. The toad-fucking Turk always wins. So why am I reclining on my stomach like this, Dick?"

Captain Gringo didn't answer. The delayed fuse he'd lit in the post armory did. The night sky turned brilliant orange. The earth rippled in shock waves under them. Then the sound waves roared over, hurting everyone's ear drums and making the adelitas scream, unheard, above the thunderous rumble of exploding dynamite, Mills bombs and ammunition. Including four-inch shells they'd had hidden in the back.

As the last rumbles echoed away and the earth stopped quivering like jelly under them, the sky stayed ruby and amber to their north. Captain Gringo said, "The pricks didn't win this time. Everything that didn't blow to smithereens is burning like hell back there."

He got to his feet. As Gaston rose, the Frenchman observed, "Nobody should suffer burns. The concussion alone must have killed everyone within a quarter mile of your naughty surprise, and the post was only two hundred meters across at best. Shall we dash on through the night now?"

Captain Gringo grinned and said, "Hell, from here on we can *stroll*. We'll go down the cuesta by moonlight and camp on the first nice rise we spot near moondown. The map says it should take us two or three days to reach Greytown. Our fake safe-conduct passes may work if we need to show them to anyone. I doubt we will. Who should question a couple of blancos in a British seaport if they pay cash and don't hang around long? Oh, yeah, here's your share of the cash I swiped from the trading post before I lit a delayed-action fuse to the armory next door!!"

As they rose and waved the girls on down the trail, Gaston grinned with delight and said, "You are becoming such a comfort to me in my old age. But let us not dash too hastily down the primrose path to Greytown, my sneaky child. We have six adorable girls to share as well. I imagine three nights on the trail ought to work out nicely for one and all, hein?"

Captain Gringo laughed and said, "I'm getting tired of lust in the dust. I'm not greedy, either. Unless you want to fight a duel over her, I was planning on checking into a nice Greytown hotel with Gordita and, hmm, maybe that skinny one called Ynez, if I can get the two of them to join me in an interesting experiment in contrast.''

Gaston frowned and said, ''Merde alors, you dare to say you are not greedy? That only leaves four pour moi!''

The Best of Adventure
by RAMSEY THORNE

"THE KING OF THE WESTERN NOVEL" IS *MAX BRAND*

___BROTHERS ON THE TRAIL	(C90-302, $1.95)
___GUNMAN'S GOLD	(C90-619, $1.95)
___HAPPY VALLEY	(C90-304, $1.75)
___LUCKY LARRIBEE	(C94-456, $1.75)
___RETURN OF THE RANCHER	(C90-309, $1.95)
___RUSTLERS OF BEACON CREEK	(C30-271, $1.95)
___FLAMING IRONS	(C30-260, $1.95)
___BULL HUNTER	(C30-231, $1.95)
___RIDER OF THE HIGH HILL	(C30-607, $1.95)
___MISTRAL	(C90-316, $1.95)
___THE SHERIFF RIDES	(C90-310, $1.95)
___SILVERTIP'S CHASE	(C98-048, $1.50)
___SILVERTIP'S ROUNDUP	(C90-318, $1.95)
___SILVERTIP'S STRIKE	(C98-096, $1.50)
___SLOW JOE	(C90-311, $1.95)
___THE STRANGER	(C94-508, $1.75)
___TAMER OF THE WILD	(C94-334, $1.75)
___WAR PARTY	(88-933, $1.50)

5 EXCITING ADVENTURE SERIES MEN OF ACTION BOOKS

___NINJA MASTER
by Wade Barker
Committed to avenging injustice, Brett Wallace uses the ancient Japanese art of killing as he stalks the evildoers of the world in his mission.
___#5 BLACK MAGICIAN   (C30-178, $1.95)
___#7 SKIN SWINDLE   (C30-227, $1.95)
___#8 ONLY THE GOOD DIE   (C30-239, $2.25, U.S.A.)
        (C30-695, $2.95, Canada)

___THE HOOK
by Brad Latham
Gentleman detective, boxing legend, man-about-town, The Hook crossed 1930's America and Europe in pursuit of perpetrators of insurance fraud.
___#1 THE GILDED CANARY   (C90-882, $1.95)
___#2 SIGHT UNSEEN   (C90-841, $1.95)
___#5 CORPSES IN THE CELLAR   (C90-985, $1.95)

___S-COM
by Steve White
High adventure with the most effective and notorious band of military mercenaries the world has known—four men and one woman with a perfect track record.
___#3 THE BATTLE IN BOTSWANA   (C30-134, $1.95)
___#4 THE FIGHTING IRISH   (C30-141, $1.95)
___#5 KING OF KINGSTON   (C30-133, $1.95)

___BEN SLAYTON: T-MAN
by Buck Sanders
Based on actual experiences, America's most secret law-enforcement agent—the troubleshooter of the Treasury Department—combats the enemies of national security.
___#1 A CLEAR AND PRESENT DANGER   (C30-020, $1.95)
___#2 STAR OF EGYPT   (C30-017, $1.95)
___#3 THE TRAIL OF THE TWISTED CROSS   (C30-131, $1.95)
___#5 BAYOU BRIGADE   (C30-200, $1.95)

___BOXER UNIT—OSS
by Ned Cort
The elite 4-man commando unit of the Office of Strategic Studies whose dare-devil missions during World War II place them in the vanguard of the action.
___#3 OPERATION COUNTER-SCORCH   (C30-128, $1.95)
___#4 TARGET NORWAY   (C30-121, $1.95)